Tsstu had come back into her arms, her claws caught in Charis's already slitted tunic. Chris regarded the curl-cat with a smile.

"We had better finish this flitting about soon or you will have me reduced to rags. Shall we try it?"

"—reee—" Agreement by mind-touch, eager anticipation. Tsstu appeared to have no doubts that they would go somewhere.

Charis stared down at the pattern.

Cold—no light at all—a terrible emptiness. Life was not. She wanted to scream under a tortue which was not of body but of mind. Lantee—where *was* Lantee? Dead? Was this death into which she had followed him?

Cold again—but another kind of cold. Light—light which carried the promise of life she knew and understood. Charis fought down the churning sickness which had come from that terror of the place where life did not exist.

A rank smell, a growling answered by Tsstu's "rrruuugh" of warning . . .

ANDRE NORTON
ORDEAL IN OTHERWHERE

ace books
A Division of Charter Communications Inc.
1120 Avenue of the Americas
New York, N.Y. 10036

First Ace printing: December, 1969
Second Ace printing: February, 1973

Printed in U.S.A.

1

CHARIS crouched behind the stump, her thin hands pressed tight to the pain in her side. Her breath came in tearing gasps which jerked her whole body, and her hearing was dimmed by the pounding blood in her ears. It was still too early in the morning to distinguish more than light and dark, shadow and open. Even the blood-red of the spargo stump was gray-black in this predawn. But it was not too dark for her to pick out the markers on the mountain trail.

Though her will and mind were already straining ahead for that climb, her weak body remained here on the edge of the settlement clearing, well within reach—within reach. Charis fought back the panic which she still had wit enough to realize was an enemy. She forced her trembling body to remain in the shadow of the stump, to be governed by her mind and not by the fear which was a fire eating her. Now she could not quite remember when that fear had been born. It had ridden her for days, coming to its full blaze yesterday.

Yesterday! Charis strove to throw off the memory of yesterday, but that, too, she forced herself to face now. Blind panic and running; she dared not give in to either or she was lost. She knew the enemy and she had to fight, but since a trial of physical strength was out of the question, this meant a test of wits.

As she crouched there, striving to rest, she drew upon memory for any scraps of information which might mean weapons. The trouble had begun far back; Charis knew a certain dull wonder at why she had not realized before *how* far back it had begun. Of course, she and her father had expected to be greeted by some suspicion—or at least some wariness when they had joined the colonists just before takeoff on Varn.

Ander Nordholm had been a government man. He and his daughter were classed as outsiders and strangers by the colony group, much as were the other representatives of law from off-world—the Ranger Franklyn, Post Officer Kaus and his two guards, the medical officer and his wife. But every colony had to have an education officer. In the past too many frontier-world settlements had split away from the Confederation, following sometimes weird and dangerous paths of development when fanatics took control, warped education, and cut off communications with other worlds.

Yes, the Nordholms had expected a period of adjustment, of even semi-ostracization since this was a Believer colony. But her father had been winning them over—he had! Charis could not have deceived herself about that. Why, she had been invited to one of the women's "mend" parties. Or had it been a blind even then?

But this—this would never have happened if it had not been for the white death! Charis's breath came now in a real sob. There were so many shadows of fear on a newly opened planet. No safeguard could keep them all from striking at the fragile life of a newly planted colony. And here had been waiting a death no one could see, could meet with blaster or hunting knife or even the medical knowledge her species had been able to amass during centuries of space travel, experimentation, and information acquired across the galaxy.

And in its striking, the disease had favored the fanatical prejudices of the colonists. For it struck first the resented government men. The ranger, the port captain and his men, her father—Charis's fist was at her mouth, and she bit hard upon her knuckles. Then it struck the medic—always the men. Later the colonists—oddly enough, those who had been most friendly with the government party—and only the men and boys in those families.

The ugly things the survivors had said—that the government was behind the plague. They had yelled that when they burned the small hospital. Charis leaned her forehead against the rough stump and tried not to remember that. She had been with Aldith Lasser, the two of them trying to find some meaning in a world which in two weeks had taken husband and father from them and turned their kind into mad people. She would not think of Aldith now; she would not! nor of Visma Unskar screaming horrors when Aldith had saved her baby for her—

Charis's whole body was shaking with spasms she could not control. Demeter had been such a fair world. In the early days after their landing, Charis had gone on two expeditions with the ranger, taking the notes for his reports. That was what they had held against her in the colony—her education, her equality with the government men. So—Charis put her hands against the stump and pulled herself up—so now she had three choices left.

She could return; or she could remain here until the hunt found her—to take her as a slave down to the foul nest they were fast making of the first human settlement on Demeter; or somehow she could reach the mountains and hide out like a wild thing until sooner or later some native peril would finish her. That seemed much the cleaner way to end. Still steadying herself with one hand on the stump, Charis stooped to pick up the small bundle of pitiful remnants she had grubbed out of the ruins of the government domes.

7

A hunting knife, blackened by fire, was her only weapon. And there were formidable beasts in the mountains. Her tongue moved across dry lips, and there was a dull ache in her middle. She had eaten last when? Last night? A portion of bread, hard and with the mustiness of mold on it, was in the bag. There would be berries in the heights. She could actually see them—yellow, burstingly plump—hanging so heavy on willowy branches that they pulled the boughs groundward. Charis swallowed again, pushed away from the stump, and stumbled on.

Her safety depended upon what the settlers would decide. She had no means of concealing her back trail. In the morning it would be found. But whether their temper would be to follow her, or if they would shruggingly write her off to be finished by the wild, Charis could not guess. She was the one remaining symbol of all Tolskegg preached against—the liberal off-world mind, the "unfemale," as he called it. The wild, with every beast Ranger Franklyn had catalogued lined up ready to tear her, was far better than facing again the collection of cabins where Tolskegg now spouted his particular brand of poison, that poison, bred of closed minds, which her father had taught her early to fear. And Visma and her ilk had lapped that poison to grow fat and vigorous on it. Charis weaved on along the trail.

There was no sign of a rising sun, she realized some time later. Instead, clouds were thicker overhead. Charis watched them in dull resignation, awaiting a day of chill, soaking rain. The thickets higher up might give her some protection from the full force of a steady pour, but they would not keep out the cold. Some cave or hole into which she could crawl before full exposure weakened her to the point that she could go no farther—

She tried to remember all the features of this trail. Twice she had been along it—the first time when they had cut the trace, the second time when she had taken the little ones to the spring to show them the wonderful sheaths of red flowers and the small, jeweled, flying lizards that lived among those loops of blossoming vines.

The little ones . . . Charis's cracked lips shaped a grimace. Jonan had thrown the stone which had made the black bruise on her arm. Yet, on that other day, Jonan had stood drinking in the beauty of the flowers.

Little ones and not so little ones. Charis began to reckon how many boys had survived the white death. All the little ones, she realized with some wonder, were still alive—that is, all under twelve years. Of those in their teens, five remained, all representing families who had had least contact with the government group, been the most fanatical in their severance. And of adult men . . . Charis forced herself to recall every distorted face in the mob bent on destruction, every group she had spied upon while hiding out.

Twenty adult men out of a hundred! The women would go into the fields, but they could not carry on the heavy work of clearing. How long would it take Leader Tolskegg to realize that, in deliberately leading the mob to destroy the off-world equipment, he might also have sentenced all of the remaining colonists to slow death?

Of course, sooner or later, Central Control would investigate. But not for months was any government ship scheduled to set down on Demeter. And by that time the whole colony could be finished. The excuse of an epidemic would cover the activities of any survivors. Tolskegg, if he *were* still alive then, could tell a plausible tale. Charis was sure that the colony leader now believed he and his people were free from the government

9

and that no ship would come, that the Power of their particular belief had planned this so for them.

Charis pushed between branches. The rain began, plastering her hair to her head, streaming in chill trickles down her face, soaking into the torn coat on her shoulders. She stooped under its force, still shivering. If she could only reach the spring. Above that was broken rock where she might find a hole.

But it was harder and harder for her to pull herself up the rising slope. Several times she went down to hands and knees, crawling untitl she could use a bush or a boulder to pull upright once more. All the world was gray and wet, a sea to swallow one. Charis shook her head with a jerk. It would be so easy to drift into the depths of that sea, to let herself go.

This was real—here and now. She could clutch the bushes, pull herself along. Above was safety; at least, freedom of a sort still undefiled by the settlers. And here was the spring. The curtain of blossoms was gone, seed pods hung in their place. No lizards, but something squat and hairy drank at the pool, a thing with a long muzzle that looked at her from a double set of eyes, coldly, without fear. Charis paused to stare back.

A purple tongue flicked from the snout, lapped at the water in a farewell lick. The creature reared on stumpy hind feet, standing about three feet tall; and Charis recognized it, in this normal pose, as one of the tree-dwelling fruit eaters that depended upon overdeveloped arms and shoulders for a method of progress overhead. She had never seen one on the ground before, but she thought it harmless.

It turned with more speed than its clumsy build suggested and used the vines for a ladder to take it up out of her sight. There was a shrill cry from where it vanished and the sound of more than one body moving away.

Charis squatted by the pool side and drank from her cupped hands. The water was cold enough to numb her palms, and she rubbed them back and forth across the front of her jacket when she was finished, not in any hopes of drying them but to restore circulation. Then Charis struck off to the left where the vegetation gave way to bare rock.

How long it was, that struggle to gain the broken country, Charis could not have told. The effort stripped her of her few remaining rags of energy, and sheer, stubborn will alone kept her crawling to the foot of an outcrop, where a second pillar of stone leaned to touch the larger and so formed a small cup of shelter. She drew her aching body into that and huddled, sobbing with weakness.

The pain which had started under her ribs spread now through her whole body. She drew her knees up to her chest and wrapped her arms about them, resting her chin on one kneecap. For a long moment she was as still as her shaking body would allow her to rest. And it was some time later that she realized chance had provided her with a better hideout than her conscious mind had directed.

From this niche and out of the full drive of the rain, Charis had a relatively unobstructed view of the downslope straight to the field on which their colony ship had first set down. The scars of its deter-rockets were still visible there even after all these months. Beyond, to her right, was the straggle of colony cabins. The dim gray of the storm lessened the range of visibility, but Charis thought she could see a trail or two of smoke rising there.

If Tolskegg was following the usual pattern, he had

already herded the majority of the adults into the fields in that race for planting. With the equipment destroyed, it would be a struggle to get the mutated seed in the ground in time for an early harvest. Charis did not move her head. From here the fields were masked by the rounded slope; she could not witness the backbreaking toil in progress there. But if the new ruler of the colony was holding to schedule, she need not fear the trailers would be early on her track—if they came at all.

Her head was heavy on her knee; the need for sleep was almost as great as the ache of hunger. She roused herself to open her bundle and take out the dry bread to gnaw. The taste almost made her choke. If she had only had warning enough to hide some of the trail rations the explorers had used! But by the time she had nursed her father to the end, the main stores had largely been raided or destroyed because of their "evil" sources.

As she chewed the noisome mouthful, Charis watched downtrail. Nothing moved in the portion of the settlement she could see. Whether or not she wanted to, whether or not it was safe, she must rest. And this was the best hole she could find. Perhaps the steady rain would wash away the traces she had left. It was a small hope but all she had left to cling to.

Charis thrust the rest of the bread back into her bundle. Then she strove to wriggle deeper into her half-cave. Spray from the rain striking the rocks reached her in spite of her efforts. But finally she lapsed into quiet, her forehead down on her knees, her only movements the shivers she could not control.

Was it sleep or unconsciousness which held her, and for how long? Charis rose out of a nightmare with a cry, but any sound she made was swallowed up by a roar from outside.

She blinked dazedly at what seemed to be a column of fire reaching from earth to gray, weeping sky. Only for a moment did that last, and then the fire was at ground level, boiling up the very substance of the soil. Charis scrambled forward on hands and knees, shouting but still blanketed by that other sound.

There was a spacer, a slim, scoured shaped, pointing nose to sky, the heat of its deter-rocket fire making a steam mist about it. But this was no vision—it was real! A spacer had set down by the village!

Charis tottered forward. Tears added to the rain, wet on her cheeks. There was a ship—help—down there. And it had come too soon for Tolskegg to hide the evidence of what had happened. The burned bubble domes, all the rest—they would be seen; questions would be asked. And she would be there to answer them!

She lost her footing on a patch of sleek clay, and before she could regain her balance, Charis was skidding down, unable to stop her fall. The sick horror lasted for an endless second or two. Then came a sudden shock, bringing pain and blackness.

Rain on her face roused Charis again. She lay with her feet higher than her head, a mass of rubble about her. Panic hit her, the fear that she was trapped or that broken bones would immobilize her, away from the wonderful safety and help of the ship. She must get there—now!

In spite of the pain, she wriggled and struggled out of the debris of the slide, crawled away from it. Somehow she got to her feet. There was no way of telling how long she had lain there and the thought of the ship waiting drove her on to make an effort she could not have faced earlier.

No time to go back to the spring trail—if she could

reach it from this point. Better straight down, with the incline of the slope to keep her going in the right direction. She had been almost directly above and behind the landing point when she had sheltered among the rocks. She must have slid in the right direction, so she only had to keep on going that way.

Was it a Patrol ship, Charis wondered as she stumbled on. She tried to remember its outline. It was certainly not a colony transport—it was not rotund enough; nor was it a regulation freighter. So it could only be a patrol or a government scout landing off-schedule. And its crew would know how to deal with the situation here. Tolskegg might already be under arrest.

Charis forced herself to cut down her first headlong pace. She knew she must not risk another fall, the chance of knocking herself out just when help was so near. No, she wanted to walk in on her own two feet, to be able to tell her story and tell it clearly. Take it slowly: the ship would not lift now.

She could smell the stench of the rocket-burn, see the steam as a murky fog through the trees and brush. Better circle here; it no longer mattered if Tolskegg or his henchmen sighted her. They would be afraid to make any move against her.

Charis wavered out of the brush into the open and started for the village without fear. She would show up on the vistaplates in the ship, and none of the colonists would risk a hostile move under that circumstance.

So—she would stay right here. There was no sign of anyone's coming out of the village. Of course not! They would be trying to work out some plausible story, whining to Tolskegg. Charis faced around toward the ship and waved vigorously, looking for the insignia which would mark it Patrol or Scout.

There was none! It took a moment for that fact to make a conscious impression on her mind. Charis had been so sure that the proper markings would be there that she had almost deceived herself into believing that she sighted them. But the spacer bore no device at all. Her arm dropped to her side suddenly as she saw the ship as it really was.

This was not the clean-lined, well-kept spacer of any government service. The sides were space-dust cut, the general proportions somewhere between scout and freighter, with its condition decidedly less than carefully tended. It must be a Free Trader of the second class, maybe even a tramp—one of those plying a none-too-clean trade on the frontier worlds. And the chances were very poor that the commander or crew of such would be lawfully engaged here or would care at all about what happened to the representatives of government they were already aligned against in practice. Charis could hope for no help from such as these.

A port opened and the landing ramp snaked out and down. Somehow Charis pulled herself together, she turned to run. But out of the air spun a rope, jerking tight about her arms and lower chest, pulling her back and off her feet to roll, helplessly entangled, a prisoner. While behind she heard the high-pitched, shrill laughter of Tolskegg's son, one of the five boys who had survived the epidemic.

II

SHE MUST keep her wits, she must! Charis sat on the backless bench, her shoulders braced against the log wall, and thought furiously. Tolskegg was there and Bag-roof, Sidders, Mazz. She surveyed what now must be the ruling court of the colony. And then, the trader. Her attention kept going back to the man at the end of the table who sat there, nursing a mug of quaffa, eyeing the assembly with a spark of amusement behind the drooping lids of his very bright and wary eyes.

Charis had known some Free Traders. In fact, among that class of explorer-adventurer-merchant her father had had some good friends, men who carried with them a strong desire for knowledge, who had added immea-surably to the information concerning unknown worlds. But those were the aristocrats of their calling. There were others who were scavengers, pirates on occasion, raiders who took instead of bargained when the native traders of an alien race were too weak to stand against superior off-world weapons.

"It is simple, my friend." The trader's insolent tone to Tolskegg must have cut the colonist raw, yet he took it because he must. "You need labor. Your fields are not going to plow, plant, and reap themselves. All right, in freeze I have labor—good hands all of them. I had my pick; not one can't pull his weight, I promise you. There was a flare on Gonwall's sun, they had to evacuate to Sallam, and Sallam couldn't absorb the excess population. So we were allowed to recruit in the refugee camp. My cargo's prime males—sturdy, young, and all under in-definite contracts. The only trouble is, friend, what do you have to offer in return? Oh—" his hand went up to silence the beginning rumble from Tolskegg. "I beg of you, do not let us have again this talk of furs. Yes, I have seen them, enough to pay for perhaps three of *my* cargo. Your wood does not interest me in the least. I want small things, of less bulk, a money cargo for a fast

16

turnover elsewhere. Your furs for three laborers—unless you have something else to offer."

So that was it! Charis drew a deep breath and knew there was no use in appealing to this captain. If he had shipped desperate men on indefinite labor contracts, he was no better than a slaver, even though there was a small shadow of legality to his business. And his present offer was sheer torment to Tolskegg.

"No native treasures—gems or such?" the captain continued. "Sad that your new world has so few resources to aid you now, friend."

Mazz was pulling at his leader's grimed sleeve, hissing into Tolskegg's ear. The frown on the other's face lightened a little.

"Give us a moment to do some reckoning, captain. We may have something else."

The trader nodded. "All the time you wish, friend. I thought that might move your memories."

Charis tried to think what Mazz had in mind. There was nothing of immediate value to trade, she was sure, save the bundle of pelts the ranger had gathered as specimens. Those had been cured to send off-world as scientific material.

The buzz of whispers among the colonists came to an end and Tolskegg faced about. "You trade in labor. What if we offer you labor in return?"

For the first time, the captain displayed a faint trace of surprise—deliberately, Charis decided. He was too old a hand at any bargaining to show any emotion unless for a purpose.

"Labor? But you are poor in labor. Do you wish to strip yourselves of what few assets you possess?"

"You deal in labor," Tolskegg growled. "And there is more than one kind of labor. Is that not so? We need strong backs, men for our fields. But there are other worlds where they may need women."

Charis stiffened. For the first time she saw more than one reason for her having been dumped here. She had thought it was merely to impress upon her the folly of hoping for any rescue. But this—

"Women?" The captain's surprise grew more open. "You would trade your women?"

Mazz was grinning, a twisted and vicious grin centered on Charis. Mazz still smarted from Ander Nordholm's interference when he had wanted to beat his wife and daughter into the fields.

"Some women," Mazz said. "Her—"

Charis had been aware that the trader had pointedly ignored her from his entrance into the cabin. To interfere in the internal affairs of any colony was against trading policy. To the captain, a girl with her arms tied behind her back, her feet pinioned, was a matter involving the settlement and not his concern. But now he accepted Mazz's statement as an excuse for giving her a measuring stare. Then he laughed.

"And of what possible value is this one? A child, a reed to break if you set her to any useful labor."

"She is older than she looks and has the learning of books," Tolskegg retorted. "She was a teacher of useless knowledge, and speaks more than one tongue. On some worlds such are useful or deemed so by the fools that live there."

"Who are you, then?" The captain spoke to her directly.

Was this a chance? Could she persuade him to take her, hoping to contact authority off-world and so obtain her freedom?

"Charis Nordholm. My father was education officer here."

"So? Oh, daughter of a learned one, what has chanced in this place?" He had slipped from Basic into the sibilant Zacathan tongue. She answered him readily in the same language.

"First, winged one, a sickness, and then the blight of ignorance."

Tolskegg's great fist struck the table with a drum thud. "Speak words we can understand!"

The captain smiled. "You have claimed for this child knowledge. I have the right to decide whether that knowledge makes her worth my buying. In the water of the north there are splinters of ice." Again he used one of the Five Tongues—that of Danther.

"But the winds of the south melt them swiftly." Charis replied to that code address almost mechanically.

"I say—speak what a man can understand. She has learning, this one. She is useless to us here. But to you she is worth at least another laborer!"

"How say you, Gentle Fem?" The trader addressed Charis. "Do you deem yourself worth a man?"

For the first time the girl allowed herself a thrust in return. "I am worth several of some!"

The captain laughed. "Well said. And if I take you, will you sign an indefinite contract?"

For a long moment Charis stared at him, her small spark of hope crushed before it had time to warm her. As her eyes met his, she knew the truth—he was not really an escape at all. This man would not take her from Demeter to someone in authority. Any bargain would be made on his terms, and those terms would bind her on almost every planet he would visit. With a labor cargo he would set down only on those worlds where such a shipment would be welcome and legal. With an indefinite contract to bind her, she could not appeal for freedom.

"That is slavery," she said.

"Not so." But his smile held almost as much malice as Mazz's grin. "To every contract there comes an end in time. Of course, you need not sign, Gentle Fem. You may remain here—if that is your wish."

"We trade her!" Tolskegg had followed this exchange with growing exasperation. "She is not one of us, nor our kind. We trade her!"

The captain's smile grew broader. "It would seem, Gentle Fem, that you have little choice. I do not think that this world will be very kind to you under the circumstances if you remain."

Charis knew he was right. Left to Tolskegg and the rest, their hatred of her the hotter for losing out on what they thought was a bargain, she would be truly lost. She drew a ragged breath; the choice was already made.

"I'll sign," she said dully.

The captain nodded. "I thought you would. You are in full possession of your senses. You—" he pointed to Mazz, "loose the Gentle Fem!"

"Already once she has run to the woods," Tolskegg objected. "Let her remain bound if you wish to control her. She is a demon's daughter and full of sin."

"I do not think she will run. And since she is about to become marketable property, I have a voice in this matter. Loose her now!"

Charis sat rubbing her wrists after the cords were cut. The captain was right—her strength and energy were gone; she could not make a break for freedom now. Since the trader had tested her education to a small degree, it was possible that learning *was* a marketable commodity for which he already foresaw profit. And to be off-world, away from Demeter, would be a small measure of freedom in itself.

"You present a problem." The captain spoke to her again. "There is no processing station here, and we cannot ship you out in freeze—"

Charis shivered. Most labor ships stacked their cargo in the freeze of suspended animation, thus saving room, supplies, all the needs of regular passengers. Space on board a trader ship was strictly limited.

"Since we lift without much cargo," he continued, "you'll bunk in the strong room. And now—what's the matter—are you sick?"

She had striven to rise, only to have the room whirl about her with a sickening lurch of floor and ceiling.

"Hungry." Charis clutched at the nearest hold, the arm the captain had put out involuntarily when she swayed.

"Well, that can be remedied easily enough."

Charis remembered little of how she got to the spacer. She was most aware of a cup pushed into her hands, warm to her cold palms, and the odor which rose from it. Somehow she managed to get the container to her lips and drink. It was a thick soup, savory, though she could not identify any of its contents. When she had finished, she settled back on the bunk and looked about the room.

Each Free Trader had a cabin with extra security devices intended to house particularly rich, small cargo. The series of cupboards and drawers about her were plainly marked with thumbprint locks which only the captain and his most trusted officers could open. And the bunk on which she sat was for a port-side guard when such were needed.

So she, Charis Nordholm, was no longer a person but valuable cargo. But she was tired, too tired to worry, to even think, about the future. She was tired—

The vibration of the walls, the bunk under her, were a part of her body, too. She tried to move and could not; panic caught at her until she saw that the webbing of the take-off belts laced her in. Thankful, Charis touched the release button and sat up. They were off-planet, headed toward what new port of call? She almost did not want to know.

Since there was no recording of time in the treasure cabin, Charis could portion hours, days, only by the clicking of the tray which brought her food through a hatch at intervals—long intervals, for the food was mostly the low-bulk, high-energy tablets of emergency rations. She saw no one and the door did not open. She might have been imprisoned in an empty ship.

At first Charis welcomed the privacy, feeling secure in it. She slept a lot, slowly regaining the strength which had been drained from her during those last weeks on Demeter. Then she became bored and restless. The drawers and cupboards attracted her, but those she could open were empty. At the fifth meal-period there was a small packet beside her rations, and Charis opened it eagerly to find a reader with a tape threaded through it.

Surprisingly enough, the tape proved to be one of the long epic poems of the sea world of Kraken. She read it often enough to commit long passages to heart, but it spurred her imagination to spin fantasies of her own which broke up the dull apathy induced by her surroundings. And always she could speculate about the future and what it might hold.

The captain—odd that she had never heard his name —had hers now, along with her thumbprint, on his contract. She was signed and sealed to a future someone else would direct. But always she could hope that chance would take her where she could appeal for aid and freedom. And Charis was very sure now that a future off-world would be better than any on Demeter.

She was reciting aloud her favorite passage from the saga when a loud clang, resounding from the walls of the cabin, sent her flat on the bunk, snapping the webbing in place. The spacer was setting down. Was this the end of the trip for her or just a way stop? She endured the pressure of planeting and lay waiting for the answer.

Though the ship must be in port, no one came to free her, and as the moments passed she grew impatient, pacing back and forth in the cabin, listening for any sound. But, save that the vibration had ceased, they could as well have been in space.

Charis wanted to pound the door, scream her desire to be out of what was now not a place of security but a cage. By stern effort she controlled that impulse. Where were they now? What was happening? How long would this continue—this being sealed away? Lacing her fingers tightly together, she went back to the bunk, willed herself to sit there with an outward semblance of patience. She might be able to communicate through the ration hatch if this went on.

She was still sitting when the door opened. The captain stood there with a bundle under his arm which he tossed to the bunk beside her.

"Get into this." He nodded curtly at the bundle. "Then come!"

Charis pulled at the fastening of the bundle to unroll a coverall uniform, the kind worn by spacemen off duty. It was clean and close enough to her size to fit if she rolled up sleeves and pants legs. Using the pocket-sized refresher of the cabin, she made a sketchy toilet, glad to discard her soiled and torn Demeter clothing. But she had to keep her scuffed and worn boots. Her hair was shoulder-length now, its light brown strands fair against her tanned skin, curling up a little at the ends. Charis drew it back to tie with a strip of cloth, forming a bobbing tail at the back of her head. There was no need to consult any mirror; she was no beauty by the standards of her race and never had been. Her mouth was too wide, her cheekbones too clearly defined, and her eyes—a pale gray—too colorless. She was of Terran stock, of middle height which made her taller than some of the mutated males, and altogether undistinguished.

But she was feminine enough to devote several seconds making sure the coverall fitted as well as she could manage and that she made the best appearance possible under the circumstances. Then, a little warily, she tried the door, found it open, and stepped out onto the level landing.

The captain was already on the ladder; only his head and shoulders were in sight. He beckoned impatiently to her. She followed him down for three levels until they came to the open hatch from which sprang the door ramp.

Outside was a glare of sunlight which made Charis blink and raise her hands to shield her eyes. The captain caught her elbow and steered her ahead into a harsh warmth, desert-like in its baking heat. And as her eyes adjusted she saw that they had indeed set down in a wasteland.

Sand, which was a uniform red outside the glassy slag left by the rocket blast, lapped out to the foot of a range of small hills, the outline of which shimmered in heat waves. There was no sign of any building, no look of a port, save for the countless slag scars which pecked and pitted the surface of the desert sand, evidence of many landings and take-offs.

There were ships—two, three, a fourth farther away. And all of them, Charis saw, were of the same type as the one she had just left, second- and third-class traders. This seemed to be a rendezvous for fringe merchants.

The captain's hold on her arm left Charis no time to examine her surroundings more closely; he was pulling rather than guiding her to the next ship, a twin to his own. And a man, with an officer's winged cap but no uniform except nondescript coveralls, stood waiting for them at the foot of the ramp.

He stared at Charis intently as she and the captain approached. But the stare was impersonal, as if she were not a woman or even a human being at all, but a new tool of which the stranger was not quite sure.

"Here she is." The captain brought Charis to a stop before the strange officer.

His stare held for a moment and then he nodded and turned to go up the ramp. The other two followed. Once inside the ship, Charis, sandwiched between the two men, climbed the core ladder up to the level of the commander's cabin. There he signaled for her to sit at a swing-down desk, pushed a reader before her.

What followed was, Charis discovered, an examination into her ability to keep accounts, her knowledge of

25

X-tee contact procedures, and the like. In some fields she was very ignorant, but in others she appeared to satisfy her questioner.

"She'll do." The stranger was very sparing of words.

Do for what? The question was on the tip of Charis's tongue when the stranger saw fit to enlighten her.

"I'm Jagan, Free Trader, and I've a temporary permit for a world named Warlock. Heard of it?"

Charis shook her head. There were too many worlds; one could never keep up with their listing.

"Probably not—back of beyond," Jagan had already added. "Well, the natives have a queer system. Their females rule, make all off-world contacts; and they don't like to deal with males, even strangers like us. So we have to have a woman to palaver with them. You know some X-tee stuff and you've enough education to keep the books. We'll put you at the post, and then they'll trade. I'm buying your contract, and that's that. Got it, girl?"

He did not wait for her to answer, but waved her away from the desk. She backed against the cabin wall and watched him thumbprint the document which transferred her future into his keeping.

Warlock—another world—unsettled by human beings except at a trading post. Charis considered the situation. Such trading posts were visited at intervals by officials. She might have a chance to plead her case before such an inspector.

Warlock— She began to wonder about that planet and what might await her there.

III

"IT's SIMPLE. You discover what they want and give it to them for as near your price as you can get." Jagan sat at the wall desk, Charis on a second pull-seat by the wall. But the captain was not looking at her; he was staring at the cabin wall as if the answer to some dilemma was scratched there as deeply as a blaster ray could burn it. "They have what we want. Look here—" He pulled out a strip of material as long as Charis's forearm and as wide as her palm.

It was fabric of some type, a pleasant green color with an odd shimmer to its surface. And it slipped through her fingers with a caressing softness. Also, she discovered, it could be creased and folded into an amazingly small compass, yet would shake out completely unwrinkled.

"That's waterproof," Jagan said. "They make it. Of what we don't know."

"For their clothing?" Charis was entranced. This had the soft beauty of the fabulously expensive Askra spider silk.

"No, this fabric is used commonly to package things—bags and such. The Warlockians don't wear clothing. They live in the sea as far as we know. And that's the only thing we've been able to trade out of them so far. We can't get to them—" He scowled, flipping record tapes about the top of his desk. "This is our chance, the big one, the one every trader dreams of having someday—a permit on a newly opened world. Make this spin right and it means—" His voice trailed off, but Charis understood him.

Trading empires, fortunes, were made from just such chances. To get at the first trade of a new world *was* a dream of good luck. But she was still puzzled as to how Jagan had achieved the permit for Warlock. Surely one of the big Companies would have made contact with Survey and bid in the rights to establish the first post. Such plums were not for the fringe men. But it was hardly tactful under the circumstances to ask Jagan how he had accomplished the nigh to impossible.

She had been spending a certain period of each ship's day with Jagan, going over the tapes he considered necessary for her briefing. And Charis had, after her first instruction hour, realized that to Jagan she was not a person at all, but a key with which he might unlock the mysteriously shut door of Warlockian trade. Oddly enough, while the captain supplied her with a wealth of information about his goods, the need for certain prices and profits, the mechanics of trading with aliens, he seemed to have very little to say about the natives themselves, save that they were strongly matriarchal in their beliefs, holding males in contempt. And they had been wary of the post after a first curious interest in it.

Jagan was singularly evasive over why the first contact had failed so thoroughly. And Charis, treading warily, dared not ask too many questions. This was like forsaking a well-worn road for a wilderness. She still had a little knowledge to guide her, but she had to pick a new path, using all her intuition.

"They have something else." Jagan came out of the thoughtful silence into which he had retreated. "It's a tool, a power. They travel by it." He rubbed one hand across his square chin and looked at Charis oddly as if daring her to take his words lightly. "They can vanish!"

"Vanish?" She tried to be encouraging. Every bit of information she could gain she must have.

"I saw it." His voice sank to a mumble. "She was right there—" one finger stabbed at the corner of the cabin, "and then—" He shook his head. "Just—just gone! They work it some way. Get us the secret of how they do that and we won't need anything else."

Charis knew that Jagan believed in the truth of what he had seen. And aliens *had* secrets. She was beginning to look forward to Warlock more than for just a chance of being free of this spacer.

But when they did planet, she was not so certain once again. The sky of mid-afternoon was amber, pure gold in places. The ship had set down among rough cliffs of red and black which shelved or broke abruptly to the green sea. Except for that sea and the sky, Warlock appeared a somber world of dark earth, a world which, to Charis, repelled rather than invited the coming of her species.

On Demeter the foliage had been a light, bright green, with hints of yellow along stem or leaf edge. Here it held a purple overcast, as if it were eternally night-shadowed even in the full sun of day.

Charis had welcomed and fiercely longed for the fresh air of the open, untainted by spacer use. But after her first tasting of that pleasure, she was more aware of a chill, a certain repulsion. Yet the breeze from the sea was no more than fresh; the few odors it bore, while perhaps strange, were not offensive in any way.

There was no settlement, no indication except for slag scars, that any spacer had finned in here before. She followed Jagan down the ramp, away from the rocket steam, to the edge of a cliff drop, for they had landed on a plateau well above sea level. Below was an inlet running like a sharp sword thrust of sea into the land. And at its innermost tip bubbled the dome of the post, a gray dome of quickly hardened plasta-skin—the usual temporary structure on a frontier planet.

"There she is." Jagan nodded. But it seemed to Charis that he was in no hurry to approach his gate to fortune. She stood there, the breeze tugging at her hair and the coveralls they had given her. Demeter had been a frontier world, alien, but until after the white death had struck it had seemed open, willing to welcome her kind. Was that because it had had no native race? Or because its very combination of natural features, of sights, sounds, smells, had been more attuned to Terran stock? Charis had only begun to assess what made that difference, trying to explore the emotions this first meeting with Warlock aroused in her, when Jagan moved.

He lifted a hand to summon her on and led the way down a switchback trail cut into the native rock by blaster fire. Behind she could hear the voices of his crew as they formed a line of men to descend.

The foliage had been thinned about the post, leaving a wide space of bare, blue soil and gray sand ringing the bubble, an elementary defense precaution. Charis caught the scent of perfume, looked into a bush where small lavender-pink balls bobbed and swung with the wind's touch. That was the first light and delicate thing she had seen in this rugged landscape.

Now that she was on a level with the post, she saw that the dome was larger than it looked from above. Its surface was unbroken by any windows; visa-screens within would be set to pick up what registered on sensitive patches of the walls. But at the seaward end there was the outline of a door. Jagan fronted that and Charis, alert to any change in the trader's attitude, was sure he was puzzled. But his pause was only momentary. He strode forward and slapped his palm against the door as if in irritation.

The portal split open and they were inside the large foreroom. Charis looked about her. There was a long table, really only a flat surface mounted on easily assembled pipelegs. A set of shelves, put together in a like manner and now occupied by a mass of trade goods, followed the curve of the dome wall along, flanking the door, and added to the portion cutting this first chamber off from the rest.

There was a second door midway of that inner wall; the man who stood there must be Gellir, Jagan's cargomaster and now post keeper. He had the deep tan of a space man, but his narrow face, with its sharp jet of chin and nose, bore signs of fatigue. There were lines bracketing his lips, dark smudges under his eyes. He was a man who was under a strain, Charis thought. And he carried a stunner, not holstered at his belt as all the crew wore them when planetside, but free in his hand, as if he expected not his captain but some danger he was not sure he could meet.

"You made it." His greeting was a flat statement of fact. Then he sighted Charis and his expression tightened into one that she thought, with surprise, was a mingling of fear and repulsion. "Why—" He stopped, perhaps at some signal from Jagan the girl had not seen.

"Through here," the captain spoke to her quickly. She was almost pushed past Gellir into a passage so narrow that the shoulders of her escort brushed the plasta walls.

He took her to the end of that way where the dome began to curve down overhead and then opened another door. "In here," he ordered curtly.

Charis went in, but as she turned, the door was already shut. Somehow she knew that if she tried to separate it by palm pressure, it would be locked.

With growing apprehension Charis looked about the room. There was a folding cot against the slope of the wall—she would have to move carefully to fit in under that curve. A stall fresher occupied a considerable space in the room where the roof was higher. For the rest, there was a snap-down table and a pull-out seat to fit beneath it and, at the foot of the cot, a box she guessed was to hold personal possessions.

More like a cell than living quarters in its design to conserve space. But, she thought, probably equal to any within the post. She wondered how big a staff Jagan thought necessary to keep here. Gellir had been in charge while the captain was off-world, and he could have been alone, a situation which would cause him to be jumpy under the circumstances. Normally a spacer of the Free Trader class would carry—Charis reckoned what she did know about such ships—normally a captain, cargomaster, assistant pilot-navigator, engineer and his assistant, a jet man, a medico, a cook—perhaps an assistant cargomaster. But that was a fully tstaffed ship, not a fringe tramp. She thought there had been four men on board beside Jagan.

Think things out, assemble your information before you act. Ander Nordholm had been a systematic thinker and his training still held in the odd turn her life had taken. Charis pulled out the seat and folded her hands on the table surface as she sat down to follow her father's way of facing a problem.

If she only knew more about Jagan! That he was desperately intent upon this project she could understand. Success meant a great deal for a fringe tramp; the establishment of a post on a newly opened planet was a huge step up. But—how had one on the ragged edge of respectability gotten the franchise for such a post in the beginning? Or—Charis considered a new thought—or had Jagan broken in here without a license? Suppose, just suppose, he had seen the chance to land well away from any government base, start trading. Then, when he was located by a Patrol from whatever headquarters did exist on Warlock, he could present an established fact. With the trade going, he could pay his fine and be left alone, because the situation could be so delicate locally that the legal representatives would not want the natives to have any hint of dissension between two off-world groups.

Then a time lapse in establishing proper contact with the aliens *would* goad Jagan into action. He would have to take any short cut, make any move he could devise, to get started. So, he needed her—

But that meeting on the desert of the unknown world where she had been traded from the labor ship to Jagan —What was that place and why had Jagan been there? Just to pick her up—or some other woman? An illegal meeting place where traders in contraband exchanged cargoes—of that she was sure. Smugglers operated all over space. A regular stop for the labor ship and Jagan was there, waiting on the chance of their carrying a woman for sale?

Which meant she had been taken by an illegal trader. Charis smiled slowly; she could be lucky because this trade had gone through. Somewhere on Warlock there was a government base where all contacts between off-worlders and natives were supervised. If she could reach that base and protest an illegal contract, she might be free even with Jagan holding her signature and thumb-print against her!

For the time being she would go along with Jagan's trading plans. Only—if the captain were working against time—Suddenly Charis felt as cold as she had when crouched on the Demeter mountainside. She was only a tool for Jagan; let that tool fail and . . .

She took an iron grip on herself, fought the cold inside her which was a gathering storm to send her beating at the door of what might be a trap. Her hands were palm-down on the table, their flesh wet. Charis strove to master the sickness in her middle and then she heard movements. Not in this cell—no—but beyond its wall.

A pounding—now heavy, now hardly more than a tapping—at irregular intervals. She was straining to hear more when the sound of metallic space-boot plates clicking against the flooring made her tense. Coming here?

She slipped sidewise on the seat to face the door. But that did not open. Instead, she heard another sound from beyond the wall—a thin mewling, animal-like, yet more frightening than any beast's cry. A human voice—low; Charis could not make out any words, just a man's tone close to the level of a whisper.

Now the sound of footsteps just without her own door. Charis sat very still, willing herself into what she hoped was the outer semblance of calm. Not Jagan entered as the door split open, but one of the crew she did not recognize. In one hand he carried a sack-bag such as the crew used for personal belongings, which he tossed in the general direction of her cot. In the other, he balanced a sealed, hot ration tray which he slid on to the table before her. The room was so small he need hardly step inside the door to rid himself of both burdens.

34

Charis was ready to speak, but the expression on his face was forbidding and his movements were those of a man in a hurry. He was back and gone, the door sealed behind him before she could ask a question.

A finger-tip pressure released the lid of the tray and Charis savored the fragrance of stew, hot quaffa. She made a quick business of eating, and her plate was cleared before she heard more sounds. Not the thumping this time but a low cry which was not quite a moan.

As suddenly as that plaint began, it stopped and there was silence. A prisoner? A member of the crew ill? Charis's imagination could supply several answers, but imagination was not to be relied upon.

As the silence continued, Charis rose to investigate the bag on the cot. Jagan or someone had made a selection of trade goods, for the articles which spilled out were items intended to catch the eye of an alien or primitive. Charis found a comb with the back set in a fanciful pattern of bits of crystal; a mirror adorned to match; a box containing highly scented soap powder, the too strong perfume of which made her sniff in fastidious disgust. There were several lengths of cloth in bright colors; a small hand-sew kit; three pairs of ornamented sandals in different sizes for a fitting choice; a robe, which was too short and too wide, of a violent blue with a flashy pattern of oblak birds painted on it.

Apparently the captain wished her to present a more feminine appearance than she now made wearing the coveralls. Which was logical considering her duties here —that she register as a woman with the natives.

Suddenly Charis yielded to the desire to be just that again—a woman. The colonists of Demeter had been a puritanical sect with strong feelings concerning the wrongness of frivolous feminine clothing. Suiting themselves outwardly as well as they could to the people they must live among, all members of the government party not generally in uniform had adapted to the clumsy, drab clothing the sect believed fitting. Such colors as now spilled across the cot had been denied Charis for almost two years. While they were not the ones she would have chosen for herself, she reached out to stroke their brightness with an odd lightening of spirit.

There were no patterns by which to cut, but she thought she had skill enough to put together a straight robe and skirt, a very modified version of the colony clothing. The yellow went with the green in not too glaring a combination. And one pair of sandals did fit.

Charis set out the toilet articles on the table, piled the material and the robe on the chair. Of course, they must have brought her the least attractive and cheapest of their supplies. But still—she remembered the strip of native material Jagan had shown her. The color of that was far better than any of these garish fabrics. Someone who used that regularly would not be attracted by what she had here. Perhaps that was one of the points which had defeated Jagan so far; his wares were not fitted to the taste of his customers. But surely the captain was no amateur; he would know that for himself.

No—definitely she would not combine the yellow with the green after all. One color alone and, if there was not enough material, Jagan would have to give her the run of his shelves to make a better selection. If she was going to represent her race before alien females, she must appear at her best.

Charis measured the length of green against her body. Another modification of the cut she had planned might do it.

"Pretty—pretty—"

She swung around. That sibilant whisper was so startling that Charis was badly shaken. The figure in the slit of the opened door whipped through and drew the portal tight shut behind her as she stood, facing Charis, her back to the door, her lips stretched in a frightening caricature of a smile.

IV

THE NEWCOMER was of a height with Charis so they could match eye to eye as they stood there, Charis gripping the fabric length tightly with both hands, the other woman continuing to laugh in a way which was worse than any scream. She must have been plump once, for her skin was loose in pouches and wrinkles on her face and in flabby flaps on her arms. Her black hair hung in lank, greasy strings about her wrinkled neck to her hunched shoulders.

"Pretty." She reached out crooked fingers and Charis instinctively retreated, but not until those crooked nails caught in the material and jerked at it viciously.

The stranger's own garments were a bundle of stuffs— a gaudy robe much like the one Charis had been given, pulled on crookedly over a tunic of another and clashing shade. And she wore the heavy, metal-plated boots of a space man.

"Who are you?" Charis demanded. Oddly enough, something in her tone appeared to awaken a dim flash of reason in the other.

"Sheeha," she replied as simply as a child. "Pretty." Her attention returned again to the fabric. "Want—" She snatched, ripping the length from Charis's grasp. "Not to the snakes—not give to the snakes!" Her lips drew flat across her teeth in an ugly way and she retreated until her shoulders were once more set against the door panel, the material now wreathed and twisted in her own claw hands.

"The snakes won't get this pretty?" she announced. "Even if they dream. No—not even if they dream . . ."

Charis was afraid to move. Sheeha had crossed the border well into a country for which there was no map of any sane devising.

"They have dreamed," Sheeha's croak of a voice was crooning, "so many times they have dreamed—calling Sheeha. But she did not go, not to the snakes, no!" Her locks of hair bobbed as she shook her head vigorously. "Never did she go. Don't you go—never—not to the snakes."

She was busy thrusting the material she had balled into a wad into a bag in her robe. Now she looked beyond Charis at the blue robe on the cot, reaching out for that, also.

"Pretty—not for the snakes—no!"

Charis snatched the garment up and pushed it into that clawing hand.

"For Sheeha—not the snakes," she agreed, trying to keep her fear from showing.

Again the woman nodded. But this time as she took the robe, she caught at Charis with her other hand, linking fingers tight about the girl's wrist. Charis was afraid to struggle. But the touch of the other's dry, burning skin against her own made her flesh shrink, and a shudder ran through her.

"Come!" Sheeha ordered. "Snakes will get nothing. We shall make sure."

She jerked Charis toward her as she swung around. The door-slit opened and Sheeha pulled the unresisting girl out into the corridor. Dared she call for help? Charis wondered. But the grasp on her wrist, the strength the other displayed, was a warning against centering Sheeha's attention on her.

As far as Charis could see, the trading post was deserted save for the two of them. The doors along the hall were shut, but that to the store was open and the light there beckoned them on. It must be early evening. Was Sheeha going out into the night? Charis, remembering the broken country about the perimeter of the post, had hopes of escape there if she could break the hold the other had on her.

But it appeared that Sheeha was bound no farther than the outer room where the shelves were crowded with the trade wares. As her eyes settled on that wealth of miscellaneous goods, she did drop her hold on Charis.

"Not to the snakes!"

She had moved down the corridor at a rapid shuffle, as if the weight of the space boots had been a handicap. But now she fairly sprang at the nearest shelf on which stood rows of small glass bottles, sweeping her arms along to send them smashing to the floor. A cloud of overpowering and mingled scents arose. Not content with clearing them from the shelves, Sheeha was now stamping on the shards which survived the first crash, her cry of "Not to the snakes!" becoming a chant.

"Sheeha!"

She had finished with the bottles and was now grabbing at rolls of materials, tearing at the stuff with her claws. But her first assault had brought a response from the owner of the post. Charis was brushed aside with a force which sent her back against the long table as Jagan burst in from the corridor and hurled himself at the frantic woman, his arms clamping hers tight to her body though she threshed and fought in his grasp, her teeth snapping as her head turned back and forth trying for a wolfish-fang grip on her captor. She was screaming, high, harsh, and totally without mind.

Two more men came on the run, one from outside, the other—whom Charis recognized as the one who had brought her the food—from the corridor. But it took all three of them to control Sheeha.

She cried as they looped a length of the unrolled fabric about her, imprisoning her arms against her body, making her into a package.

"The dreams—not the dreams—not the snakes!" The words broke from her as a plea.

Charis was surprised to see the emotion on Jagan's face. His hands rested gently on Sheeha's shoulders as he turned her around to face, not the interior corridor of the post but the outer door.

"She goes to the ship," he said. "Maybe there . . ." He did not complete that sentence but, steering the woman before him, he went out into the night.

The overwhelming odors of the spilt perfumes were thick enough to make Charis sneeze. Trails of trade fabrics cascaded down from the second shelf Sheeha had striven to clean off. Mechanically Charis went over to loop the material up from the mess on the floor, circling about the glass shards which were still visible in the powder Sheeha's boots had ground.

"You—" She glanced up as the man by the table spoke. "You'd better go back now."

Charis obeyed, glad to be out of the wreckage. She was shivering as she sat down upon her cot once again, trying to understand what had happened. Jagan said he needed a woman to contact the natives. But before Charis's coming there had already been a woman here —Sheeha. And that Sheeha was to the captain something more than a tool Charis was sure, having watched his handling of her frenzy.

The snakes—the dreams? What had moved Sheeha to her wild talk and acts? Charis's own first impression of Warlock, that it was not a world to welcome her kind— was that the truth and not just a semiconscious, emotional reaction to certain landscape coloring? What *was* happening here?

She could go out, demand an explanation. But Charis discovered that her will this time was not strong enough to make her cross that threshold again. And when she did try the door and found she could not open it, she sighed in relief. In this small cell she felt safe; she could see every inch of it and know she was alone.

The light from the glow-track running along the ceiling of the bubble was growing dimmer. Charis deduced they were slacking power for the night. She curled up on the cot. Odd. Why was she so sleepy all at once? There was a flicker of alarm at her realization at that oddness. Then . . .

Light again, all around her. Charis was aware of that light even though her eyes were closed. Light and warmth. Then came the desire to know from whence they reached her. She opened her eyes and looked up into a serene, golden sky. *Golden* sky? She had seen a golden sky—where? when? A part of her pushed away memory. It was good to lie here under the gold of the sky. She had not rested so, uncaring, for a long, long time.

A tickle at her toes, a lapping about her ankles, up around her calves. Charis stirred, used her elbows to prop herself up. She lay in warm, gray sand in which there

41

were small, glittering points of red, blue, yellow, green. Her body was bare, but she felt no need for any clothing; the warmth was covering of a sort. And she lay on the very verge of a green sea with its foremost wavelets lapping gently at her feet and legs. A green sea . . . As with the golden sky, that triggered memory, memory which something within her feared and fought.

She was languorous, relaxed, happy—if this freedom could be called happiness. This was right! Life should always be a clear gold sky, a green sea, jeweled sand, warmth, no memories—just here and now!

Save for the kiss and go of the waves there was no movement. Then Charis wanted more than this flaccid content and sat up. She turned her head to find that she was in a pocket of rock with a steep red cliff behind and about her and, seemingly, no path out. Yet that did not disturb her in the least. With her fingers she idly shifted the sand, blinking at the winks of color. The water was washing higher, up to her knees now, but she had no wish to withdraw from its warm caress.

Then—all the languor, the content, vanished. She was not afraid, but aware. Aware of what? one part of her awakening mind demanded. Of what? Of—of an intelligence, another awareness. She scrambled up from the sand which had hollowed about her body and stood, this time giving the rock walls about her a closer examination. But there was nothing there, nothing save herself stood alive in this pocket cup of rock and sand.

Charis looked to the sea. Surely there—right there— was a troubling of the water. Something was emerging, coming to her. And she . . .

Charis gasped, gasped as if the air could not readily fill too empty lungs. She was on her back, and it was no longer gold day but dim pale night about her. To her right was the curve of the bubble wall. She could barely make it out, but her outflung hand proved it solid and real. But—that sand had also been real as it had shifted between her fingers. The soft lap of the sea water, the sun and air on her skin? They, too, had been real.

A dream—more vivid and substantial than any she had ever known before? But dreams were broken bits of things, like the shards Sheeha had left on the floor of the trade room. And this had not been broken, contained nothing which did not fit. That awareness at the end, that belief that there was something rising from the sea to meet her?

Was it that which had broken the dream pattern, brought her awake and into that frightening sense, for a fraction of a second, that she was drowning—not in the sea which had welcomed and caressed her but in something which now lay between the realization of that sea and this room?

Charis wriggled off the cot and padded to the seat by the table. She was excited, experiencing the sensation which she had known when she anticipated some pleasure yet to come. Would a second try at sleep return her to the sea, the sand, the place in space and time where something—or someone—awaited her?

But the sensation of well-being which she had brought with her from the dream, if dream that had been, was seeping away. In its place flowed the same vague discomfort and repugnance which had claimed her from her first leaving the spacer. Charis found herself listening, as it seemed, not only with her ears but with every part of her.

No sound at all. Without knowing exactly why, she went to the door. There was still light from the roof, dimmed to twilight but enough to see her way around.

Charis set her hands on either side of the slit and applied pressure. And the portal opened, allowing her to look down the corridor.

This time she faced no string of closed doors; they all gaped open. Again she listened, trying to still her own breathing. What did she expect to hear? A murmur of voices, the sound of some sleeper's heavy intake and expulsion of air? But there was nothing at all.

Earlier her room had seemed a haven of safety, the only security she could hope to find. Now she was not so sure, just as she could not put name to the intangible atmosphere which made her translate her growing uneasiness into action she could not have assayed before.

Charis started down the hall. Her bare feet made no sound on the floor which was too chill as she paused at the first door. That was open wide enough to show her another cot—empty, just as the room was empty. The second room, more sleeping quarters without a sleeper. A third room with the same deserted bareness. But the fourth room was different. Even by this dim light she could make out one promising feature, a com visa-screen against the far wall. There was a table here, two chairs, a pile of record tapes. Ugly, distorted—

She was startled into immobility. It was almost as if she had seen this room and its furnishings through eyes which measured and disdained it and all it stood for. But that odd dis-orientation had been only a flash, the visa-screen drew her. It was undoubtedly set there to be a link between a planeting ship and the post. But, too, it might just furnish her with a key to freedom. Somewhere on Warlock there was a government base. And this com could pick up that station, would pick if up if she had the patience and time to make a sweep-beam search. Patience she could produce; time was another

44

matter. Where were the traders? All back to the spacer for some reason? But why?

Where earlier she had crept, now Charis sped, making the round of the post: the sleeping rooms—all empty; the cook unit with its smell of recently heated rations and quaffa still lingering but otherwise closed tight; the larger outer room, where the smashed glass had been brushed into a pile and then left, where one strip of tangled and creased material still fluttered from a hastily wrapped roll; back to the com room. She was alone in the post. Why and for how long she could not tell, but for the moment she *was* alone.

Now it was a matter of time, luck, and distance. She could operate the sweep, set its probe going to pick up any other com-beam within a good portion of planet surface. If this was the middle of a Warlockian night, there might be no one on duty at the government base com. Still she could set a message to be picked up on its duty tape, a message which would bring the authorities here and give her a chance to tell her story.

Pity she could not increase the glow of lights, but she had not found the control switch. So Charis had to lean very close to the keyboard of the unit to pick out the proper combination to start the sweep.

For a moment or two Charis was bewildered by a strange and unorthodox arrangement of buttons. Then she understood. Just as the ship Jagan captained was certainly not new or first class, this was a com of an older type than any she had seen before. And a small worry dampened her first elation. What *would* be the range of sweep on such an antiquated installation? If the government base was too far away, she might have little hope of a successful contact.

Charis pressed the button combination slowly, intent

upon making no error in setting up a sweep. But the crackles of sound which the activated beam fed back into the room was only the natural atmospheric response of an empty world. Charis had heard that on Demeter the times she had practiced the same drill.

Only the beep-beep spark traveling from one side of a small scan-plate to the other assured her that the sweep was active. Now she had nothing to do but wait, either to catch another wave or face the return of the traders.

Having set the com to work, Charis returned to her other problem. Why had she been left alone in the station at night? From the deeply cleft valley of the inlet she could not see the landing site of the plateau where the spacer had planeted. Jagan had taken Sheeha to the ship, but he had left at least two men here. Had they believed her safely locked in her room so they could leave for some other necessary duty? All she knew of the general routine of the post she had learned from the captain, and that had been identical to the cramming of what he had wanted her to know of his business.

The faint beeping of the sweep was a soothing monotone, too soothing. Charis's head jerked as she shook herself fully awake. One third of the circle had registered no pick-up, and at least a fourth of the circumference must be largely sea, from which direction she could expect no positive response.

That came just when Charis was almost convinced there was no hope for her, it came—weak, so weak that the distance must be great. But she had a direct beam on it and so could increase receptive volume. Somewhere to the northeast, another off-world com was beaming.

Charis's fingers flew, centering her sweep, adding to its intensity. The visa-plate before her clouded, began to

46

clear again. She was picking up an answer! Charis reacted more quickly than she had thought possible as
some instinct sent her dodging to one side, away from the
direct line of the plate and so out of sight—or at least out
of focus—for a return cast.

The figure which emerged from the clearing mist was
no government man, though he *was* a man or at least
humanoid in appearance. He wore the same dingy coveralls as the traders used; belted at his thick waist was not
the legal stunner but a highly illegal blaster. Charis's hand
shot out and thumbed the lever which broke connection
just as the expression of open surprise on his face turned
to one of searching inquiry.

Breathing fast, the girl crept back to her place before
the screen. Another post—somewhere to the north. But
the blaster? Such a weapon was strictly forbidden to anyone except a member of the Patrol or Defense forces. She
hesitated. Dare she put the sweep to work again? Try it
south? She had not recognized the man pictured on the
plate as one of the ship's crew, but still he could be one
of Jagan's men. And so the captain's actions here could
be more outside the law than she had guessed.

Standing well to one side of the screen, Charis triggered the sweep again. Moments later she had a pick-up
to the south. However, what flashed on the screen this
time was no armed space man but a very familiar standby
pattern—the insignia of Survey surmounted by a small
Embassy seal, signifying an alien contact mission manned
by Survey personnel. There was no operator on duty;
the standby pattern clarified that. But they would have a
pick-up tape ready to record. She could send a message
and know that it would be read within hours. Charis
began to click out the proper code words.

V

A SOFT SWISH of sound, a light touch on her body.

Charis looked about her with an acceptance which was in itself part of the strangeness of this experience. She had been huddled in the seat before the com, beating out on its keys her call for attention. Then—she was here, back somehow in the dream.

But, she knew a second or so later after the dawn of that realization, this was not quite the same dream after all. She wore the coverall she had pulled on before she began her night's prowling of the deserted post. Her bare feet sent small messages of pain along nerves and she glanced down at them. They were bruised and there was a scrape along one instep which oozed drops of blood. Instead of that feeling of oneness and satisfaction she had had before, now she was tired and confused.

There, as it had before, rolled the sea under the light of morning. And about her were rocky cliffs, while her sore feet sank into loose and powdery sand. She was on the shore—there was no doubting that, but this could not be a dream.

Charis turned, expecting to see the post on its narrow tongue of water, but behind her was a cliff wall. She could sight a line of depressions in the sand, ending at the point where she now stood, marking her trail, and those led back out of sight. Where she was and how she had come here she did not know.

Her heart picked up the beat of fear, her breath came

faster in shallow gasps. She could not remember. No forcing of thought could bring back memory.

Back? Maybe she could trace her way back along her trail. But even as she turned to try that, Charis found she could not. There was a barrier somehow, a sensation almost as keen as physical pain, which kept her from retracing. Literally she could not take the first step back. Shaking, Charis faced around and tried again to move. And the energy she expended nearly sent her sprawling on her face. If she could not return, there was nothing to prevent her going forward.

She tried to equate the points of the compass. Had she strayed north or south from the post? She thought south. South—the government base lay to the south. If she kept on, she had a chance of reaching that.

How small that chance might be Charis dared not consider. Without supplies, without even shoes, how long could she keep going? Some wild thoughts troubled her. Had she brought this upon herself because she had striven to contact the base by com? She cupped her hands over her eyes and stood, trying to understand, trying to trace the compulsion which must have led her to this place. Had her conscious mind blanked out? Her need for escape, for reaching the government base, had that then taken over? It made sense of a sort, but it had also led her into trouble.

Charis limped down to the sea and sat on a rock to inspect her feet. They were bruised, and there was another cut on the tip of a toe. She lowered them into the water and bit her lip against the sting of the liquid in her wounds.

This might be a world without life, Charis thought. The golden-amber sky held floating clouds, but no birds or winged things cut across its serenity. The sand and rocks about her were bare of any hint of growing things, and there was no break on the smooth surface of the beach save the hollows of her own footprints.

Charis pulled open the seal front of her coverall and took off her undershirt. It was a struggle to tear that, but at the cost of a broken nail she at last had a series of strips which she bound about her feet. They would be some protection since she could not remain where she was forever.

Some hundred feet or so to the south, the cliff pointed out to meet the sea with no strip of easily traveled beach at its foot. She would have to climb there. But Charis sat where she was for a while, marking the hand- and-foot-holds to use, when she had to.

She was hungry—as hungry as she had been back on the mountain on Demeter, and there was not even a hunk of bread for her this time. Hungry and thirsty— although the water washed before her mockingly. To go on into a bare wilderness was sheer folly, yet there was that invisible barrier on the back trail. Now, even to turn her head and retrace by eye the hollow sand prints required growing effort.

Grimly she rose on her bandaged foot and limped to the cliff. She could not stay there, growing weaker with hunger. There could be hope that beyond the cliff there was more than just sand and rock.

The climb taxed her strength, scraped her palms and fingers almost as badly as her feet. She pulled out on the pitted surface of the crest and lay with her hands tight against her breast, sobbing a little. Then she raised her head to look about.

She had reached the lip of another foliage-choked, narrow valley such as the one which held the trading post. But here were no buildings, nothing but trees and brush. However, not too far away a thread of water splashed down to make a stream flowing seaward. Charis licked dry lips and started for that. Within seconds she crouched on blue earth, her hands tingling in the chill of the spring water as she drank from cupped palms, not caring whether her immunization shots, intended for any lurking danger on Demeter, would hold on Warlock.

If the sea beach had been empty of life, the same was not true of this valley. Her thirst assuaged, Charis squatted back on her heels and noticed a gauzy-winged flying thing skim across the water. It rose again, a white thread-like creature writhing in the hold of its two pincer-equipped forelegs, and was gone with its victim between a bush and the cliff wall.

Then, from over her head, burst a clap of sound as if someone had brought two pieces of bone sharply together. Another flyer, a great deal more substantial and a hundred times larger than the insect hunter, shot out of a hole in the cliff and darted back and forth over her. The thing had leathery skin-wings, its body naked of any feathers or fur, the hide wrinkled and seamed. The head was very large in proportion and split halfway down its length most of the time as an enormous fang-set mouth uttered "clak-clak" noises.

A second flyer joined the first, then a third, and the racket of their cries was deafening. They swooped lower and lower and Charis's first curiosity turned to real alarm. One alone would have been no threat, but a flock of the things, plainly set upon her as a target for their dives, could mean real trouble. She looked about for cover and plunged in under the matted branches of the stunted-tree grove.

Apparently her passage was not hidden from the clakers even though they could not reach her, for she could hear their cries following her as she moved toward the sea. Something leaped up from just before her and squealed as it ran for the deeper shadows.

Now she hesitated, unsure of what else might lie in this wood—waiting. The smell of growing things—some pleasant, some disagreeable to her off-world senses—was strong here. Her foot came down on a soft object which burst before she could shift her weight and she saw a mashed fruit. More of these hung from the branches of the tree under which she stood and lay on the ground where the squealing creature had been feeding.

Charis plucked one and held it to her nose, sniffing an unfamiliar odor which she could not decide was pleasant or the reverse. It was food, but whether she could eat it was another question. Still holding the fruit, Charis pushed on seaward.

The clamor of the clakers had not stilled but kept pace with her progress, yet the open water tugged at her with a queer promise of safety. She came to the last screen of brush from which the vegetation straggled on to vanish in a choke of gray sand.

There was a smudge on the horizon which was more, Charis believed, than a low-flying cloud bank. An island? She was so intent upon that that she did not, at first, note the new activity of the clakers.

They were no longer circling about her but had changed course, flying out to sea where they wheeled and wove aerial patterns over the waves. And there was a disturbance in those same waves, marking action below their surface. Something was coming inshore, heading directly toward her.

Charis unconsciously squeezed the fruit until its squashed pulp oozed between her fingers. Judging by the traces, the swimmer—who or what that might be—was large.

But she did not expect nightmare to splash out of the surf and face her across so narrow a strip of beach. Armor plate in the form of scales, greened by clinging seaweed laced over the brown serrations, a head which was also armed with hornlike extensions projecting above each wide eye, a snout to gape in a fang-filled mouth . . .

The creature clawed its way up out of the wash of the waves. Its legs ended in web-jointed talons. Then it whipped up a tail, forked into two spike-tipped equal lengths, spattering water over and ahead. The clakers set up a din and scattered, soaring up, but they did not abandon the field to the sea monster. But the creature paid them no attention in return.

At first Charis was afraid it had seen her, and when it did not advance she was temporarily relieved. A few more waddling steps brought it out of the water, and then it flattened its body on the sand with a plainly audible grunt.

The head swung back and forth and then settled, snout resting outstretched on the scaled forelegs. It had all the appearance of desiring a nap in the warmth of the sun. Charis hesitated. Since the clakers had directed their attention to the fork-tail they might have forgotten her. It was the time to withdraw.

Her inner desire was to run, to crash back into the brush and so win from the valley, which had taken on the semblance of a trap. But wisdom said she was to creep rather than race. Still facing the beast on the shingle, Charis retreated. For some precious seconds she thought her hope was succeeding. Then . . .

The screech overhead was loud, summoning. A claker spied her. And its fellows screamed in to join it. Then

Charis heard that other sound, a whistling, pitched high to hurt her ears. She did not need to hear those big feet pounding on the shingle or the crackle of broken brush to know that the fork-tail thing was aroused and coming.

Her only chance now was the narrow upper end of the valley where the cliff wall might give her handholds to rise. Bushes raked and tore at her clothing and skin as she thrust through any thin spot she could sight. Past the spring and its draining brook she staggered to a glade where lavender grass grew thickly, twisted about her feet, whipping blood from her with sharp leaf edges.

Always above, the clakers screamed, whirled, dived to get at her, never quite touching her head but coming so close that she ducked and turned until she realized that she was losing ground in her efforts to evade their harassing. She threw herself into the cover on the other side of that open space, using her arm as a shield to protect her face as she beat her way in by the weight of her body.

Then she was at her goal, the rock wall which rimmed the valley. But would the clakers let her climb? Charis flattened herself against the stone to look up at the flock of leather-wings from under the protection of her crooked arm. She glanced back where shaking foliage marked the sea beast moving in.

They were *all* coming down at her! Charis screamed, beat out with both arms.

Cries . . .

She flailed out defensively, wildly, before she saw what was happening. The flight of the clakers had brought them to a line which crossed the more leisurely advance of the fork-tail. And so they had run into trouble. For, as storm lightning might strike, the forked tail swept up and lashed at the flyers, hurling bodies on and out to smash against the cliff wall.

Twice that tail struck, catching the avid first wave of attackers, and then some of the second wave who were too intent upon their target or too slow to change course. Perhaps five screeched their way up into the air to circle and clak, but not to venture down again.

Charis spun around and feeling for hand- and foot-holds, began to climb. The fork-tail was now between her and the remaining clakers. Until she had reached a higher point, she might not have to fear a second attack. She centered all her energy upon reaching a ledge where some vines dropped ragged loops not far from her groping fingers.

She pushed up and into the tangle of vine growth which squashed under her squirming body, rolling over as fast as she could to look back at the enemy. The clakers were in a frenzy, rising as if wishing to skim down at her, while below, Charis cringed back.

The fork-tail was at the foot of the cliff, its webbed talons clawing at the rock. Twice it managed to gain a small hold and was able to pull up a little, only to crash back again. Either the holds were not deep enough to sustain its weight or some clumsiness hindered its climb. For it moved awkwardly, as if on land its bulk were a liability.

But its determination to follow her was plain in those continued efforts to find talon-holds on the stone. Charis sidled along the vine-grown ledge with care lest one of those loops of tough vegetation trip her. She stopped once to tear loose a small length of the stuff, using it to lash out at a claker which had gathered resolution enough to dive at her head. The whip of vine did not touch the flyer, but it did send it soaring away in haste.

She could use that defense as long as she traveled the ledge, but when she turned to climb once more, she could

55

not so arm herself. And she was approaching a point where the shelf was too narrow to afford foot room.

The fork-tail still raised on hind feet below, clawing at the cliff wall with single-minded tenacity. A slip on her part would topple her into its reach. And she dared not climb with the clakers darting at her head and shoulders. Now she could keep them off with the lashing vine, but they were growing bolder, their attacks coming closer together, so that her arm was already tired of wielding the improvised whip.

Charis leaned against the cliff wall. So far it looked as if the reptilian attacker could not reach her. But the clakers' harassment continued unbated, and she was tired, so tired that she was beginning to fear that even if they did withdraw, she would not have the strength left to finish the pull up to the top of the cliff.

She rubbed her hand across her eyes and tried to think, though the continuing din of the attackers made her feel stupid, as if her brain was befuddled and cocooned in the noise. It was the cessation of that clamor which brought her to full consciousness again.

Overhead the ugly creatures had ceased to wheel. Instead they turned almost as one and winged across the valley, to snap into the holes in the rock from which they had earlier emerged. Bewildered, the girl could only stare after them. Then, that sound from below— Steadying her body with one hand on the rock wall, Charis looked down.

The fork-tail had turned and, on four feet once again, was making a ponderous way back through the smashed and crushed growth, heading seaward without a backward glance to the ledge where she stood. It was almost as if the clakers and the sea beast had been ordered away from her . . .

What made her put that interpretation on their movements? Charis absently rubbed the rest of the sticky fruit pulp from her hand on a fibrous vine leaf. Silence —nothing stirring. The whole valley as she could now see it, save for the waving foliage where the fork-tail retreated, could have been empty of life. She must make the most of this oddly granted breathing spell.

Doggedly she set about reaching the top of the rise, expecting any moment to have the clakers burst at her. But the silence held. She stood up on the crest, looked beyond for cover.

This was a plateau much like the one Jagan had used as a landing space. Only this showed no rocket scarring. South, it stretched on as might the surface of a wall well above the sea, open to air and sun with no cover. But Charis doubted if she could descend again. So she turned south, limping on her tender feet, always listening for the clak-clak of the enemy.

A splotch of color, vivid against the dull, black-veined, deep red of the rocks. Odd that she had not seen that earlier when she first surveyed this height. It was so brightly visible now that it drew her as might a promise of food.

Food . . . Her hand come up over her eyes and fell again as she strove to make sure that this was not a hallucination but that it did exist outside of her craving hunger.

But if part of a hallucination, would not the so-pictured foods have been familiar—viands she had known on Demeter or other worlds where she had lived? This was no pile of emergency rations, no setting out of known breads, fruits, meats. On the strip of green were several round balls of a deeper green, a shining white basin filled with a yellow lumpy substance, a pile of flat rounds which were a light blue. A tablecloth spread with a meal! It *had* to be a hallucination! It could not have been there earlier or she would have seen it at once.

Charis shuffled to the cloth and looked at the objects on it. She put out a scratched and grimy hand and touched fingers to the side of the bowl to find it warm. The odor which rose from it was strange—neither pleasant nor unpleasant—just strange. She hunkered down, fighting the wild demand of her body to be fed while she considered the strangeness of this food out of nowhere. Dream? But she could touch it.

She took up one of the blue rounds, found it had the consistency of a kind of tough pancake. Rolling it into a scoop, Charis ladled up a mouthful of the yellow—was it stew? Dream or not, she could chew it, taste it, swallow it down. After that first experimental mouthful, she ate, greedily, without caring in the least about dream or reality.

VI

CHARIS FOUND the tastes were as difficult to identify as the odors—sweet, sour, bitter. But on the whole, the food was pleasant. She devoured it avidly and then ate with more control. It was not until she had emptied the bowl by the aid of her improvised pancake spoon that she began to wonder once more about the source of that feast.

Hallucination? Surely not that. The bowl about which she cupped a hand was very real to the touch, just as the food had been real in her mouth and now was warm and filling in her stomach. She turned the basin about, studying it. The color was a pure, almost radiant white; and, while the shape was utilitarian and without any ornamentation, it was highly pleasing to the eye and suggested, Charis thought, a sophistication of art which marked a high degree of civilization.

And she did not need to give the cloth a closer inspection to know that it matched the strip Jagan had shown her. So this must have all come from the natives of Warlock. But why left here—on this barren rock as if awaiting her arrival?

On her knees, the bowl still in her hands, Charis slowly surveyed the plateau. By the sun's position she guessed that the hour was well past midday, but there were no shadows here, no hiding place. She was totally alone in the midst of nowhere, with no sign of how this largesse had arrived or why.

Why? That puzzled her almost more than how. She could only believe that it had been left here for her. But that meant that "they" knew she was coming, could gauge the moment of her arrival so well that the yellow stew had been hot when she first tasted it. There was no mark that any aircraft had landed.

Charis moistened her lips.

"Please—" her own voice sounded thin and reedy and, she had to admit, a little frightened as she listened to it "—please, where are you?" She raised that plea to a call. There was no answer.

"Where are you?" Again she made herself call, louder, more beseechingly.

The echoing silence made her shrink a little. It was as if she were exposed here to the view of unseen presences —a specimen of her kind under examination. And she wanted away from here—now.

Carefully she placed the now empty bowl on the rock.

There were several of the fruit and two pancakes left. Charis rolled these up in the cloth. She got to her feet, and for some reason she could not quite understand, she faced seaward.

"Thank you." Again she dared raise her voice. "Thank you." Perhaps this had not been meant for her, but she believed that it had.

With the bundle of food in her hand, Charis went on across the plateau. At its southern tip she looked back. The shining white of the bowl was easy to see. It sat just where she had left it, exposed on the rock. Yet she had half expected to find it gone, had kept her back turned and her eyes straight ahead for that very reason.

To the south, the terrain was like a flight of steps, devised for and by giants, descending in a series of ledges. Some of these bedded growths of purple and lavender vegetation, but all of it spindly short bushes and the tough knife-bladed grass. Charis made her way carefully from one drop to the next, watching for another eruption of clakers or other signs of hostile life.

She had to favor her sore feet and that journey took a long time, though she had no way of measuring the passing of planet hours save by the sun's movements. It was necessary that she look forward for shelter against the night. The sense of well-being which had warmed her along with the food was fading as she considered what the coming of Warlockian darkness might mean if she did not discover an adequate hiding place.

At last she determined to stay where she was on the ledge she had just reached. The stubby growth could not mask any large intruder, and she had a wide view against any sudden attack. Though how she might defend herself without weapons, Charis did not know. Carefully she unwrapped the remains of the food and put it aside on some leaves she pulled from a sprawling plant. She began to twist the alien fabric into a cord, finding that its soft length did crush well in the process, so that she ended with a rope of sorts.

With a withered branch she was able to pry a stone about as big as her fist from the earth, and she worked hurriedly to knot it into one end of her improvised rope. Against any real weapon this would be a laughable defense, but it gave her some small protection against native beasts. Charis felt safer when she had it under her hand and ready for use.

The sunlight had already faded from the lower land where she now was. With the going of that brighter light, splotches of a diffused gleam were beginning to show here and there. Bushes and shrubs glowed with phosphorescence as the twilight grew deeper, and from some of them, as the heat of the day chilled away, a fragrance was carried by a rising sea breeze.

Charis settled her back against the wall of the drop down which she had come, facing the open. Her weapon lay under her right hand, but she knew that sooner or later she would sleep, that she could not keep long at bay the fatigue which weighted not only her drooping eyelids but her whole body. And when she slept . . . Things happened while one slept on Warlock! Would she awake once more to find herself in a new and strange part of the wilderness? To be on the safe side, she put the food in its leaf-wrapping into the front of her coverall and tied the loose end of the scarf weapon about her wrist. When she went this time, she would take what small supplies she had with her.

Tired as she was, Charis tried to fight that perhaps betraying sleep. There was no use speculating about what force was in power here. To keep going she must concentrate on the mechanics of living. Something had turned the clakers and the sea beast from attack. Could she ascribe that to the will of the same presence which had left the food? If so, what was "their" game?

Study of an alien under certain conditions? Was she being used as an experimental animal? It was one answer and a logical one to what had happened to her so far. But at least "they" had kept her from real harm—her left hand folded over the lump of food inside her coverall; as yet any active move on "their" part had been to her advantage.

So sleepy . . . Why fight this leaden cloud? But—where would she wake again?

On the ledge, chilled and stiff, and in a dark which was not a true dark because of those splotches of light-diffusing plants and shrubs. Charis blinked. Had she dreamed again? If so, she could not remember doing so this time. But there was some reason why she must move here and now, get down from the ledge, then get over there.

She got up stiffly, looping the scarf about her wrist. Was it night or early morning? Time did not matter, but the urgency to move did. Down—and over there. She did not try to fight that pressure but went.

The light plants were signposts for her, and she saw that either their light or scent had attracted small flying things that flickered with sparkles of their own as they winged in and out of those patches of eerie radiance. The somberness of Warlock in the day became a weird ethereality by night.

Darkness which was true shadow beyond—that was her goal. As had happened on the beach when she had struggled to turn north to try and retrace her path to the post, so now she could not fight against the influence which aimed her at that dark blot, which exerted more and more pressure on her will, bringing with it a heightening of that sense of urgency which had been hers at her abrupt awakening.

Unwillingly she came out of the half-light of the vegetation into darkness—a cave or cleft in the rock. Drifts of leaves were under her feet, the sense of enclosing walls about her. Charis's outflung hands brushed rock on either side. She could still see, however, above her the wink of a star in the velvet black of the night sky. This must be a passage then and not a true cave. But again why? *Why?*

A second light moved across the slit of sky, a light with a purpose, direction. The flying light of some aircraft? The traders searching for her? That other she had seen on the com screen? But she thought this had come from the south. A government man alerted to her message? There was no chance of being seen in the darkness and this slit. She had been moved here to hide—from danger or from aid?

And she was being held here. No effort of her struggling will could move her another step or allow her to retreat. It was like being fixed in some stiff and unyielding ground, her feet roots instead of means of locomotion. A day earlier she would have panicked, but she had changed. Now her curiosity was fully aroused and she was willing, for a space, to be governed so. She had always been curious. "Why?" had been her demanding bid for attention when she was so small she remembered having to be carried for most of the exploration journeys Ander Nordholm had made a part of her growing. "Why were those colors here and not there?" "Why did this animal build a home underground and that one in a tree?" Why?—why?—why?

He had been very wise, her father, using always her thirst for knowledge to suggest paths which had led her to make her own discoveries, each a new triumph and wonder. In fact, he had made her world of learning too perfect and absorbing, so that she was impatient with those who did not find such seeking the main occupation of life. On Demeter she had felt trapped, her "whys" there battered against an unyielding wall of prejudice and things which were and must always be. When she had fought to awaken the desire to reach out for the new among her pupils, she had clashed with a definite will-not-to-know and fear-of-learning which had first rendered her incredulous and then hotly angry and, lastly, stubbornly intent upon battle.

While her father had been alive, he had soothed her, turned her frustrated energy to other pursuits in which she had freedom of action and study. She had been encouraged to explore with the ranger, to record the discoveries of the government party, received as an equal among them. But with the settlers, she had come to an uneasy truce which had burst into open war at her father's death, her repulsion for their closed minds fanned into hatred by what had happened when Tolskegg took over and turned back the clock of knowledge a thousand years.

Now Charis, free from the frustrations of Demeter, had been presented with a new collection of whys which seemed to have restrictions she could not understand, to be sure, but which she could chew on, fasten her mind to, use as a curtain between past and present.

"I'll find out!" Charis did not realize she had spoken aloud until some trick of the dark cleft in which she stood made a hollow echo of those words. But they were no boast, a promise rather, a promise she had made herself before and always kept.

The star twinkling above was alone in the sky. Charis listened for the sound of a copter engine beat and thought that she caught such a throb, very faint and far in the distance.

"So." Again she spoke aloud, as if who or what she addressed stood within touching distance. "You didn't want them to see me. Why? Danger for me or escape for me? What do you want of me?" There was no reason to expect any reply.

Suddenly the pressure of imprisonment was gone. Charis could move again. She edged back to settle down in the mouth of the cleft, facing the valley with its weird light. A breeze shush-shushed through the foliage, sometimes setting light plants to a shimmer of dance. There was a chirruping, a hum of night creatures, lulling in its monotone. If something larger than the things flying about the light vegetation was present, it made no sound. Once again, since the urgency had left her, Charis was drowsy, unable to fight the sleep which crept up her as a wave might sweep over her body on the shore.

When Charis opened her eyes once again, sunlight fingered down to pattern the earth within reach of her hand. She rose from the dried leaf-drift which had been her bed, pulled by the sound of running water: another cliff-side spring to aid her toilet and give her drink. Her two attempts to make leaf containers to carry some of the liquid with her were failures and she had to give up that hope.

Prudence dictated a conservation of supplies. She allowed herself only one of the pancakes, now dry and tough, and two of the fruit she had brought from the feast on the plateau. Because such abundance had appeared once, there was no reason to expect it again.

The way was still south but Charis's aching muscles argued against more climbing unless she was forced to it. She returned to the cleft and found that it was indeed a passage to more level territory. The heights continued on the western side, forming a wall between the sea and a stretch of level fertile country. There was a wood to the east with the tallest trees Charis had yet seen on Warlock, their dark foliage a blackened blot which was forbidding. On the edge of that forest was a section of brush, shrub, and smaller growth which thinned in turn to grass—not the tough, sharp-bladed species she had suffered from in the valley of the fork-tail, but a mosslike carpet, broken here and there by clumps of smaller stands bearing flowers, all remarkably pale in contrast to the dark hue of leaf and stem. It was as if they were the ghosts of the more brightly colored blossoms she had known on other worlds.

The mossy sward was tempting, but to cross it would take her into the open in full sight of any hunters. On the other hand, she herself would have unrestricted sight. While in the forest or brush belt, her vision would be limited. Swinging her stone-and-scarf weapon, Charis walked into the open. If she kept by the cliff, it would guide her south.

It was warmer here than it had been by the sea. And the footing proved as soft as she had hoped. Keeping to the moss, she walked on a velvety surface which spared her bruised feet, did not tear the tattered rags of covering she had fashioned for them. Away from the dark of the wood, this stretch of Warlockian earth was the most welcoming she had found.

A flash of wings overhead made her start until she saw

that this was not a claker but a truly feathered bird, with plumage as pale as the flowers and a naked head of brilliant coral red. It did not notice Charis but skimmed on, disappearing over the cliff toward the sea.

Charis did not force the pace. Now and again she paused to examine a flower or insect. She might be coming to the end of a journey a little before her appointed time and could now spare attention for the things about her. During one rest she watched, fascinated, as a scaled creature no larger than her middle finger, walking erect on a pair of sturdy hind legs, dug with taloned front "hands" in a patch of earth with the concentration of one employed in a regular business. Its efforts unearthed two round gray globes which it brushed to one side impatiently after it had systematically flattened both. Between those spheres had been packed a curled, many-legged body of what Charis believed was a large insect. The lizard-thing straightened his find out and inspected it with care. Having apparently decided in favor of its usability, it proceeded to dine with obvious relish, then stalked on among the grass clumps, now and again stooping to search the earth with a piercing eye, apparently in search of another such find.

Midday passed while Charis was still in the open. She wondered if food would again appear in her path, and consciously watched for the gleam of a second white bowl and the fruit piled on a green cloth. However, none such was to be seen. But she did come upon a tree growing much to itself, bearing the same blue fruit which had been left for her, and she helped herself liberally.

She had just started on when a sound shattered the almost drowsy content of the countryside. It was a cry—frantic, breathless, carrying with it such an appeal for aid against overwhelming danger that Charis was startled into dropping her load of fruit and running toward the sound, her stone weapon ready. Was it really that small cry which awakened such a response in her or some emotion which she shared in some abnormal way? She only knew that there was danger and she must give aid.

Something small, black, coming in great leaps, broke from the brush wall beyond the rim of the forest. It did not head for Charis but ran for the cliff, and a wave of fear hit the girl as it flashed past. Then the compulsion which had willed against her turning north, which had held her in the cleft last night, struck Charis. But this time it brought the need to run, to keep on running, from some peril. She whirled and followed the bounds of the small black thing, and like it, headed for the sea cliff.

The black creature ran mute now. Charis thought that perhaps those first cries had been of surprise at sudden danger. She believed she could hear something behind —a snarling or a muffled howl.

Her fellow fugitive had reached the cliff face, was making frantic leaps, pawing at a too-smooth surface, unable to climb. It whimpered a little as its most agonizing efforts kept it earthbound. Then, as Charis came up, it turned, crouched, and looked at her.

She had a hurried impression of great eyes, of softness, and the shock of the fear and pleading it broadcast. Hardly aware of her act but conscious she had to do something, she snatched up the warm, furred body which half-leaped to meet her grasp and plastered itself to her, clinging with four clawed feet to the stuff of her coverall, its shivering a vibration against her.

There was a way up that she, with her superior size, could climb. She took it, trying not to scape her living burden against the rock as she went. Then she was in a fissure, breathless with her effort, and a warm tongue tip made a soft, wet touch against her throat. Charis wriggled back farther into hiding, the rescued creature cradled in her arms. She could see nothing coming out of the wood as yet.

A faint mewing from her companion alerted her as a brown shadow padded out on the lavender-green of the moss—an animal she was sure. But from this distance and height, Charis could not make it out clearly as it slunk on, using bushes for cover. So far it had not headed in their direction.

But the animal was not alone. Charis gasped. For the figure now coming from between two trees was not only humanoid—it wore the green-brown uniform of Survey. She was about to call out, to hail the stranger, when the freezing she had known in the cleft caught and held her as soundless, as motionless, as if she had been plunged into the freeze of a labor ship. Helpless, she had to watch the man walk back and forth as if searching for some trail, and at last disappear back into the wood with his four-footed companion.

They had never approached the cliff, yet the freeze which held Charis did not break until long moments after they had gone.

VII

"Meerrreee?" A soft sound with a definite note of inquiry. For the first time Charis looked closely at her fellow fugitive, meeting as searching a gaze turned up at her.

69

The fur which covered its whole body was in tight, tiny curls, satin-soft against her hands. It had four limbs ending in clawed paws, but the claws were retractable and no longer caught in her clothing. There was a short tail like a fringed flap, now tucked neatly down against the haunches. The head was round, sloping to a blunt muzzle. Only the ears seemed out of proportion to the rest. They were large and wide, set sideways instead of opening forward toward the front of the skull, and their pointed tips had small tassle-tufts of gray fur of the same color that ringed the large and strikingly blue eyes and ran in narrow lines down the inner sides of the legs and on the belly.

Those eyes— Fascinated, Charis found it difficult to look away from the eye. She was not trained in beast-empathy, but she could not deny there was an aura of intelligence about this small and appealing creature which made her want to claim a measure of kinship. Yet, for all its charm, it was not to be only cuddled and caressed; Charis was as certain of that as if it had addressed her clearly in Basic. It was more than animal, even if she was not sure how.

"Meerrreee!" No inquiry now but impatience. It squirmed a little in her hold. Once more a pale yellow tongue made a lightning dab against her skin. Charis released her grip, fearing for an instant that it would leave her. But it jumped from her lap to the rough floor of the crevice and stood looking at the forest from which its enemy had emerged.

Enemy? The Survey man! Charis had almost forgotten him. What had restrained her from hailing him? Perhaps his very being here had been the answer to her call from the post. But why had she not been allowed to meet him? For allowed *was* the proper term. A prohibition she could not explain had been laid upon her. And Charis knew, without trying such an experiment, that if she attempted to go to the wood she would not be able to push past an invisible wall someone or something had used to cut her off.

"Meeerreee?" Again a question from the furred one. It paused, one front paw slightly raised, looking back at her from the entrance to the crevice.

Suddenly Charis wanted to get out of this moss-carpeted land. The frustration of her flight from the very help she wished was sour in her. Up over the cliff wall back to the sea— The longing to be again beside the waves was a pulling pain.

"Back to the sea." She said that aloud as if the furred one could understand. She came out of the crevice and glanced up for a way to climb.

"Meeree . . ."

Charis had expected the animal to vanish into the moss meadow. Instead, it was demanding her attention in its own way before it moved sure-footedly along, angling up the surface of the cliff. Charis followed, warmed by the realization that the animal appeared to have joined forces with her, if only temporarily. Perhaps its fear of the enemy in the forest was so overpowering it wanted the promised protection of her company.

While she was not as agile as the animal, Charis was not far behind when they reached the crest of the cliff. From here one could look down on the expanse of the sea and a line of silver beach. There was a feeling of peace. Peace? For an instant Charis recaptured the feeling she had known in that first dream—contentment and peace. The animal trotted ahead, south along the cliff top. From this point the drop to the sand was too sheer to descend, so Charis again followed the other's lead.

They came down to the silver strand by a path her companion found. But when Charis would have gone on south, the Warlockian creature brushed about her ankles, uttering now and then an imperative cry, plainly wanting her to remain. At last she dropped down to sit facing the sea, and then, looking about her, she was startled. This *was* the cove of her first dream exactly.

"Meerree?" That tongue-tip touch, a sense of reassurance, a small warm body pressed against hers, a feeling of contentment—that all was well . . . coming from her companion or out of some depth within herself? Charis did not know.

They came out of the sea, though the girl had not seen them swimming in. But these were not a threat like the fork-tail. Charis drew a deep breath of wonder and delight or welcome as the contentment flowered within her. They came on, walking through the wash of the waves, then stood to look at her.

Two of them, glittering in the sun, sparkling with light. They were shorter than she, but they walked and stood with a delicate grace which Charis knew she could never equal, as if each movement, conscious or unconscious, were a part of a very ancient and beautiful dance. Bands of jewel colors made designs about each throat in gemmed collars, ran down in spirals over chest, waist, thigh, braceleting the slender legs and arms. Large eyes with verticle slits of green pupils were fixed on her. She did not find the saurian shape of their heads in the least repulsive—different, yes, but not ugly, truly beautiful in their own fashion. Above their domed, jewel-marked foreheads stood a sharp V point of spiky growth, a delicate green perhaps two shades lighter than the sea from which they had come. This extended down in two bands, one for each shoulder, wider as if aping wings.

They wore no clothing, save a belt each from which hung various small implements, and a pair of pouches. Yet their patterned, scaled skin gave the impression of rich robes.

"Meeerrrreeee!" The furred body against hers stirred. Charis could not doubt that was a cry of pleasure. But she did not need that welcome from the animal. She had no fear of these sea ones—the Wyverns surely, the masters—or rather the mistresses—of Warlock.

They advanced and Charis arose, picking up the furred one, waiting.

"You are—" she began in Basic, but a four-digit hand came out, touched her forehead between the eyes. And in that touch was not the feel of cold reptilian flesh but of warmth like her own.

No words. Rather it was a flow of thought, of feeling, which Charis's off-world mind turned into speech: "Welcome, Sister—One."

The claim of kinship did not disturb Charis. Their bodies were unlike, yes—but that flow of mind to mind —it was good. It was what she wanted now and forever.

"Welcome." She found it hard to think, not to speak. "I have come—"

"You have come. It is good. The journey has been weary, but now it will be less so."

The Wyvern's other hand moved up into the line of Charis's vision. Cupped against the scaled palm was a disk of ivory-white. And once seeing it, she found she could not look away. A momentary flash of uneasiness at that sudden control and then . . .

There was no beach, no whispering sea waves. She was in a room with smooth walls that were faintly opalescent as if they were coated with sea-shell lining. A window broke one of those surfaces, giving her a view of open sea and sky. And there was a thick mat spread under that, a covering of fluffy feathers folded neatly upon it.

"For the weary—rest."

Charis was alone except for the furred one she still held. Yet that suggestion or order was as emphatic as if she had heard the words spoken. She stumbled to the mat and lay down, drew the fluffy cover over her bruised and aching body, and then plunged into another time—world—existence . . .

There was no arbitrary measurement of time where she went, nor was memory ever sharp set enough to give her more than bits and pieces of what she experienced, learned, saw in that other place. Afterward, things she had garnered sank past full consciousness in her mind and rose in time of need when she was unaware that she held such secrets. Schooling, training, testing—all three in one.

When she awoke again in her windowed room, she was Charis Nordholm still, but also she was someone else, one who had tasted a kind of knowledge her species had never known. She could touch the fringe of that power, hold a little of it; yet the full mystery of it slipped through her fingers much as if she had tried to hold tightly the waters of the sea.

Sometimes she sensed disappointment in her teachers, a kind of exasperation, as if they found her singularly obtuse just when they hovered on the edge of a crucial revelation, and then her own denseness was a matter of anger and shame for her. She had such limitations. But yet she fought and labored against them.

Which was the dream—existence in that other world or this waking? She knew the room at times and the Citadel in the island kingdom of the Wyverns, of which it was a part, and other rooms in other places she knew were not the Citadel. She knew sea depths: Had she gone there in body or in her dream? She danced and ran along the sands of shores with companions who sported and played joyously with the same bursting sense of happy release that she knew. That, she believed, was real.

She learned to communicate with the furred one, if on a limited plane. Tsstu was her name and she was one of a rare species from the forest lands, not truly animal, not wholly "human," but a link between such as Charis's own kind had sought for years.

Tsstu and the Wyverns and their half-dream existence in which she was caught up, absorbed, in which memory faded into another and far less real dream. But there was to be an awakening as sudden and as racking as that of a warrior startled from slumber by the onslaught of the enemy.

It came during one of the periods Charis believed real, when she was in the Citadel on an island apart from the land mass where the post stood. She had been teasing her companion Gytha to share dreams with her, a process of communication which swept one wholly adrift in wonder. But the young Wyvern seemed absent-minded and Charis guessed a portion of her attention was elsewhere in rapport with her kind, whom Charis could only reach if they willed it so.

"There is trouble?" She thought her question, her hand going instinctively to the pouch at her belt in which rested her guide, the carved disk they had given her. She could use it, though haltingly, to control dangerous life such as the fork-tails or to travel. Of course, she could not draw upon the full Power; maybe she never would. Even the Wise One, Gysmay, who was a Reader of Rods, could not say yes or no on that though, in a way Charis did not understand, the elder Wyvern could read the future in part.

"Not so, Sharer of my Dreams." But even as the answer came, Gytha vanished with a will-to-Otherwise. The impression she left—Charis frowned—that faint trail of impression was of trouble, and trouble connected with herself.

She brought out her guide, felt it warm comfortingly on her palm. Practice with it—that was important. Each time she bent the Power to her will she was that much more proficient. The day was fair; she would like to be free in it. What harm in her using the disk ashore? And Tsstu had been restless. For both of them to return to the moss meadow might be enjoyable. Memory moved—the Survey man there. Somehow she had forgotten about him, just as the post and the traders had receded so far into the dreamy past that they were far less real than a shared dream.

Cupping the disk, she thought of Tsstu and then heard the answering "Meerreee" from the corridor. Charis pictured the moss meadow, questioned, and was answered with an eager assent. She caught up the small body as it bounded toward her and held it against her as she breathed upon the disk and made a new mind-picture —the meadow as she remembered it most vividly by that solitary fruit tree.

Then Tsstu wriggled out of Charis's hold, pranced on her hind legs, waving her front paws in the air ecstatically, until the girl laughed. She had not felt as young and free as this for as long as she could remember. To be Ander Nordholm's assistant had once absorbed all her interest and energy, and then there had been nothing but dark shadows until she had seen the Wyverns coming to her through the sea. But now, no Wyverns—nothing but Charis and Tsstu, removed from the need for care, in a wide and welcoming stretch of countryside.

Charis threw out her arms, put up her head, so that the warmth of the sun was directly on her face. Her hair, which always intrigued the Wyverns so, she had caught back with a tie the same green as the clinging tunic she now wore.

This time her feet were shielded from hurt with sandals of shell seemingly impervious to wear, yet as light as if she were barefoot. She felt as if she might emulate Tsstu and dance on the moss. She had taken a few tentative steps when she heard it, a sound which sent her backing swiftly into the cover of the tree branches—the hjm of an airborne motor.

A copter was coming from the southeast. In general appearance it was like any other atmosphere flyer imported from off-world. Only this one had service insignia, the Winged Planet of Survey surmounted by a gold key. It was slanting away, out to sea in the general direction of the Citadel.

In all the time she had been with the natives, they had had no contact that she had known of with any off-worlders save herself. Nor had the Wyverns ever mentioned such. For the first time Charis speculated about that. Why had she herself never asked any questions about the government base, made any attempt to get the Wyverns to take or send her there? She had seemed to forget her own species while she was with the Warlockians. And that was so unnatural that she was uneasy when she realized it now.

"Meeerrreee?" A paw patted her ankle. Tsstu had caught Charis's thought or at least her uneasiness. But the animal's concern was only partly comforting.

The Wyverns had not wanted Charis to return to her own kind. It had been their interference on her first awakening that had kept her from retracing her trail to the post, had made her take cover from the flyer in the night, avoid the Survey man. She had had only kindness —yes—and an emotion which her species could term love, and care and teaching from them. But why had they brought her here, tried to cut her off from her own blood? What use did they have for her?

Use—a cold word, and yet one her mind fastened upon now only too readily. Jagan had brought her here to use as a contact with these same wielders of strange powers. Then she had been skillfully detached from the post, led to the meeting by the sea. And understanding that, Charis broke free of the enchantment which had bound her to the Otherwhere of the Wyverns.

The copter was out of sight. Had it been summoned for her? Charis was sure not. But she could have been there when it arrived. She called Tsstu, caught her up, and concentrated upon the disk to return.

Nothing happened. She was not back in the Citadel room but still under the tree in the meadow. Again Charis set her mind to the task of visualizing the place she wanted to be and it was there, as a vivid picture in her mind, but *only* in her mind.

Tsstu whimpered, butted her head under Charis's chin; the girl's fear had spread to her companion. For the third time, Charis tried the disk. But it was as if whatever power had once been conducted through that was turned off at the source. Turned off and by the Wyverns. Charis was as certain of that as if she had been told so, but there was one way to test the truth of her guess.

She raised the disk for the fourth time, this time painting a mind-picture of the plateau top where the mysterious feast had been spread. Sea wind in her hair, rock about— She was just where she had aimed to go. So—she *could* use the disk here, but she could not return to the native stronghold.

They must have known that she had left the Citadel. They did not want her to return while the visitor was there—or ever?

One of those half messages from Tsstu which came not as words or pictures but obliquely: something wrong near here . . .

Charis looked from the sea to the slit of valley where she had seen the fork-tail, secure in her knowledge that neither the sea beast nor the clakers could attack a disk carrier. From here she could see nothing amiss below. Two clakers screeched and made for her and then abruptly sheered away and fled for their nesting holes. Charis used the disk to reach the scrap of beach below the cliff. She had forgotten to bring Tsstu but she could see the black blot against the red of the rock where the little creature was making a speedy descent.

Tsstu reached the bottom of the cliff and vanished into the cloak of vegetation. Charis moved inland, the mental call bringing her to the spring.

A broken bush, torn turf. Then, on a stone, a dark sticky smear about which flying things buzzed or crawled sluggishly. In the edge of the pool, something gleamed in a spot of sun.

Charis picked up the stunner—not just any off-world weapon but one she knew well. When Jagan had had her in his cabin on the spacer to give her those instructions in what he intended to be her duties, she had seen such a side arm many times. The inlay of cross-within-a-circle set into the butt with small black vors stones had been a personal mark. It was out of the bounds of possibility that two weapons so marked could be here on Warlock.

She tried to fire it, but the trigger snapped on emptiness; its charge was exhausted. The trampled brush, the torn-up sod, and that smear— Charis forced herself to draw her finger through the congealed mess. Blood! She was sure it was blood. There had been a fight here and, judging by the lost stunner, the fight must have gone against the weapon's owner or his weapon would not be left so. Had he faced a fork-tail? But there was no path of wreckage such as that beast had left on its pursuit of her, traces of which still remained to be seen. Only there had been a fight.

Tsstu made a sound deep in her throat, an "rrrrurrgh" of anger and warning. Moved purely by impulse, Charis caught up Tsstu and used the disk.

VIII

THE SMELL caught at Charis's throat, made her cough, even before she knew the source. This was the post clearing—just as she had aimed for—the bubble of the building rising from bare earth. Or the remains of it, for there were splotched holes in its fabric from which the plasta-cover peeled in scorched and stinking strips. Tsstu spat, growled, communication with Charis firm on the need for immediate withdrawal.

But there was a prone figure by the ragged hole which had once been a door. Charis started for that—

"Hoyyyyyy!"

She whirled, her disk ready. There was someone on

the trail which led down the cliff face. He moved faster, waving to her. She could escape at any moment she chose and that knowledge led her to stand her ground. Tsstu spat again, caught a clawed grip of Charis's tunic.

From the brush rim of the clearing came a brown animal, trotting purposefully. It walked with its back slightly arched, showing off the bands of lighter color along each side, the fur thick and long. More of the light fur was visible above its eyes. Its ears were small, its face broad, the tail bushy.

Just out of the bushes it stopped to eye Charis composedly. Tsstu made no more audible protests, but the trembling of her body, her fear of mind, was transmitted to Charis. For the second time the girl readied her disk.

The man who had waved disappeared from the trail; he must have jumped down the last few feet. Now a whistle sounded from the foliage. The brown animal squatted down where it was. Charis watched warily as the newcomer burst into the clearing in a rush.

He wore the green-brown of Survey, with the addition of high boots of a dull copper, supple material. On his tunic collar was the glint of metal—the insignia of his corps again modified with a key as it had been on the copter. He was young, though nowadays with the mixture of races and the number of mutants, planet years were hard to guess. Not as tall as the usual Terran breed though, and slender. His skin was an even brown which might be its natural shade or the result of much weathering, and the hair, rather closely cropped to his round skull was almost as tightly curled and just as black, as Tsstu's fur.

His impetuous break into the open halted and he stood staring at Charis in open disbelief. The brown animal rose and went to him, rubbing against his legs.

"Who are you?" he demanded in Basic.

"Charis Nordholm," she replied mechanically. Then she added, "That beast of yours—he frightens Tsstu—"

"Taggi? You need not fear him." The brown animal reared against the man's thigh and he fondled its head, scratched behind the small ears. "But—a curl-cat!" He was gazing now with almost as great surprise at Tsstu. "Where did you get it? And how did you make friends with it?"

"Meeerrreeee." Some of Tsstu's fear had lessened. She wriggled about in Charis's arms as if settling herself in a more comfortable position, watching both man and animal with wary interest.

"She came to me," Charis fitted the past to the present, "when you were hunting her with that animal!"

"But I never—" he began and then stopped "—oh, back in the woods that day Taggi went off on a new scent! But why—who *are* you?" His tone had a new snap; this was official business now. "And what are you doing here? Why did you hide when I searched here earlier?"

"Who are *you?*" she countered.

"Cadet Shann Lantee, Survey Corps, Embassy-Liaison," he replied almost in one breath. "You sent that message, the one entered on our pick-up tape, didn't you? You were here with the traders, though where you were just a little while ago—"

"I wasn't here. I have just come."

He moved toward her, the animal Taggi remaining where it was. Now his eyes were intent, with a new kind of measurement.

"You've been with *them!*"

And Charis had no doubt as to whom that "them" referred.

82

"Yes." She was not prepared to add to that, but he seemed to need no other answer.

"And you've just come here. Why?"

"What has happened here? That man there—" She turned toward the body once more but the Survey officer in one swift stride was blocking her view of it.

"Don't look! What's happened?—Well, I'd like to know that myself. There's been a raid. But who or why—Taggi and I have been trying to learn what could have happened here. How long have you been with *them*?"

Charis shook her head. "I don't know." It was the truth, but would this Lantee believe it?

He nodded. "Like that, eh? Some of their dreaming . . ."

It was her turn for surprise. What did this officer know of the Wyverns and their Otherwhere? He was smiling slowly, an expression which modified his usual set of mouth, made him even more youthful.

"I, too, have dreamed," he said softly.

"But I thought—!" She had a small prick of emotion which was not amazement but, oddly, resentment.

His smile remained, warm and somehow eager. "That they do not admit males can dream? Yes, that is what they told us, too, once upon a time."

"Us?"

"Ragnar Thorvald and I. We dreamed to order—and came out under our own command, so they had to give us equal status. Did they do the same to you? Make you visit the Caverns of the Veil?"

Charis shook her head. "I dreamed, yes, but I don't know about your cavern. They taught me how to use this." On impulse she held up the disk.

Lantee's smile vanished. "A guide! They gave you a guide. So that's how you got here!"

"You don't have one?"

"No, they never offered us those. And you don't ask—"

Charis nodded. She knew what he meant. With the Wyverns, you waited for their giving; you did not ask. But apparently Lantee and this Thorvald had better contact with the natives than the traders had been able to establish.

The traders—the raid here. She did not realize that she was speaking aloud her thoughts as she said:

"That man with the blaster!"

"*What* man?" Again that official voice from Lantee.

Charis told him of that strange last night in the post when she had awakened to find herself in a deserted building, of her use of the com and the answer the sweep had picked up in the north. Lantee shot questions at her, but the answers she had were so limited she could tell him little more than the fact that the stranger in the visa-plate had worn an illegal weapon.

"Jagan had a limited permit," Lantee said when she had done. "He was here on sufferance and against our recommendation, and he had only a specified time in which to prove his trade claim. We heard he had brought in a woman as liaison, but that was when he first set up the post . . ."

"Sheeha!" Charis broke in. Rapidly she added that part of the story to the rest.

"Apparently she couldn't take the dreams," Lantee observed. "They reached for her, just as they did for you. But she wasn't receptive in the right way, so it reacted on her, broke her. Then Jagan made another trip and got you. But this other crowd—the one you picked up that night—that spells trouble. It looks as if they hit here—"

Charis glanced at the body. "Is that Jagan? One of his men?"

"It's a crewman, yes. Why did you come here? You taped a call for help to escape that night."

She showed him the stunner, told him of where and how she had found it. Lantee was far from smiling now.

"The com in the post was smashed along with everything else inside that wasn't blast-burned. But—there *was* something else. Have you ever seen a mate to this before, or was it part of Jagan's stock—a keepsake?"

Lantee moved back to the body he had warned her not to approach and picked an object from the ground beside it. When he came back, he held an unusual weapon, now horribly stained for a third of its length. It had the general appearance of a spear or dart, but the sawlike projections extended farther down its shaft than was natural in a spearhead.

Charis's fingers were a tight fist about her disk as Lantee held it closer to her. The bone-white substance was very like that used in the guide.

"I never saw it before." She told the truth, but in her a fear was growing.

"But you have an idea?" He was too acute!

"Suppose, just suppose," Lantee continued, on longer holding her eye to eye as if demanding her thoughts, but regarding the strange spear with a brooding expression, "that this is native to Warlock!"

"*They* don't need such weapons," Charis flashed. "They can control any living thing through these." She waved her balled fist.

"Because they dream." Lantee noted. "But what of those of their race who do not dream?"

"The—the males?" For the first time Charis wondered about that. Now she remembered that, in all the time she had spent with the Wyverns, she had not seen any male of their species. That they existed she knew, but there appeared to be a wall of reticence surrounding any mention of them.

"But—" she could not believe in Lantee's suggestion "—that is the sign of blaster fire." With her chin she pointed to the post.

"Yes. Blaster fire, systematic wrecking of every installation—and then this—used to kill an off-worlder. It's as complicated as a dream, isn't it? But this is real, too real by far!" He dropped the stained spear to lie between them. "We have to have answers and have them quick." He looked up at her. "Can you call them? Thorvald went out to the Citadel for a conference before he knew about this."

"I tried to go back before—they'd walled me out."

"We have to know what happened here. A body with this in it. Up there—" Lantee waved toward the plateau, "—an empty ship just sitting. And out of here, as far as Taggi can trace, not a single trail. Either they lifted in by aircraft or—"

"The sea!" Charis finished for him.

"And the sea is *their* domain; there is not much happens out there that they are not aware of."

"You mean—*they* planned this?" Charis demanded coldly. To her mind violence of this kind was not the Wyvern way. The natives had their own powers and those did not consist of blaster fire and serrate-toothed spears.

"No," Lantee agreed with her promptly. "This has the stamp of a Jack job, except for that." He toed the spear. "And if a Jack crew planeted here, the sooner we combine forces against them, the better!"

To that Charis *could* agree. If Jagan's poor outfit had been fringe trading, it had still been on the side of the law. A Jack crew was a thoroughly criminal gang, pirates swooping on out-world trading posts to glut, kill, and be off again before help could be summoned. And on such an open world as Warlock, they might well consider lingering for awhile.

"You have a Patrol squad on world?" she asked.

"No. We're in a queer situation here. The Wyverns won't allow any large off-world settlement. They only accepted Thorvald and me because we did, by chance, pass their dream test when we were survivors of a Throg raid. But they wouldn't agree—or haven't yet—to any Patrol station. We have a scout that visits from time to time and that's the limit.

"This post of Jagan's was an experiment, pushed on us by some of the off-world VEEPS who wanted to see how a nongovernment penetration would be accepted. And the big Companies didn't want the gamble. That's how a Free Trader got it. There are just Thorvald, Taggi, his mate Togi and their cubs, and me, plus a com-tech generally resident at headquarters."

As if the mention of his name summoned him, the brown animal lumbered forward. He sniffed the spear and growled. Tsstu spat, her claws pricking through to Charis's skin.

"What is he?" she asked.

"Wolverine, a Terran-mutated team animal," Lantee answered a little absently. "Could you try to raise them again? I have a hunch that time is getting rather tight."

Gytha—among the Wyverns Charis had been the closest to that young witch who had shared some of her instruction—maybe she could break through by beaming the power directly at Gytha and not at the Citadel as a whole. She did not answer Lantee's question in words but breathed upon the disk, and closed her eyes the better to visualize Gytha.

At her first meeting with the Wyverns, they had had a

87

physical uniformity which made it difficult for an off-worlder to see them as individuals. But Charis had learned that their jeweled skin-patterns varied, that this adornment had meaning. The younger members of their species, when they came to adulthood and the use of the Power, could take certain simplifications of designs worn by the elders of their family lines and then gradually add the symbols of their own achievements, spelled out in no code Charis could yet understand, although by it she could now recognize one from another.

So it was easy to visualize Gytha, to beam her desire for her friend. She expected mind contact but, at an exclamation from Lantee, she opened her eyes to see Gytha herself, the gold and crimson circles about her snout agleam in the sun, the spine ridges along her back moving a little as if she had actually used them to fly here.

"He-Who-Dreams-True." The mental greeting reached out to Lantee.

"She-Who-Shares-Dreams." Charis was startled when the Survey man answered in the same way. So he did have communication with the Wyverns in spite of the fact he possessed no disk.

"You have called!" That was aimed at Charis with a sharpness which suggested her act had been an error of judgment.

"There is trouble here—"

Gytha's head turned; she surveyed the wreckage of the post, glanced once at the body.

"It does not concern us."

"Nor this either?" Lantee made no move to pick up the spear again, but with boot toe he nudged it a little closer to the Wyvern.

She looked down, and a barrier between her and Charis snapped into place, as a door might slam. But

Charis had been long enough among Gytha's kind to read the flash of agitation in the sudden quiver of the Wyvern's forehead crest. Her indifference of moments before was gone.

"Gytha!" Charis tried to break through the barrier of silence. But it was as if the Wyvern was not only deaf but that Charis and Lantee had ceased to exist. Only the bloodstained spear had reality and meaning.

The Wyvern made no gesture of warning. But they were there—two more of her kind. And one—Charis took a quick step back—one of the new arrivals had a head crest which was close to black in shade; the whole surface of her scaled skin was covered with such a multiplicity of gemmed design that she flashed Gysmay—one of the Readers of Rods!

With her came the impact, first of irritation; then, as the Wyvern looked at Lantee, a cold anger, cold enough to strike as a weapon.

Though the Survey officer swayed, his face greenish under the brown, he stood up to her. Under that momentary burst of anger, Charis caught the suggestion of surprise in the Wyvern.

The second Warlockian who had accompanied Gysmay at Gytha's summons made no move. But from her, too, flowed emotion—if one could name it that—a feeling of warning and restraint. Her head crest was also black, but there was no flashing display of patterned skin bright in the sun. At first glance Charis thought she wore no designs at all, even the "encouragement" ones of her ancestors. Then the girl noted that there was a series of markings, deceptively simple, so close in hue to the natural silver of her skin as to make a brocade effect detectable only after concentrated study.

For Lantee or Charis this newcomer had no attention

at all; she was staring unwinkingly at the spear. That rose from the spot where Lantee had dropped it, moving up horizontally on a level with the Wyvern's eyes, coming to her. Then it stopped, balanced in the air for a long moment.

It whirled end for end and dashed groundward. There was a sharp snapping as it shattered into bits. It might have been broken against rock instead of bare earth. Then the splinters whirled about and rose in turn. Charis watched unbelievingly as those needle-small remnants of the spear spun madly about. They fell, stilled, but now they formed what was surely a pattern.

The girl reeled. Tsstu, in her arms, screeched. The wolverine squalled. Charis watched Lantee collapse limply under a mental blow of rage, so raw and hot as to be a fire within one's tormented brain. There was a red cloud about her, but Charis was most aware of the pain in her head.

That pain accompanied her into the dark nibbled at her will, weakened her struggle to pull away from it. Was it pain or something behind the pain, compelling her, making her no longer Charis Nordholm but a tool to be used, a key to turn for another, stronger personality?

The pain pushed at her. She crawled through a red haze—on and on. Where? for what purpose? There was only the whip of pain and the need to obey that other will which wielded such a lash. Red, red, all about her. But the red was fading slowly as a fire falls into ash. Red to gray, gray which remained about her, a gray she could see . . .

Charis lay on her back. There was an arch of wall close to her right hand; it sloped inward over her head. She had seen that wall before. Half-light so dim—bare walls—a drop table—a seat by it. The trading post—she was back in the trading post!

IX

IT WAS oddly still. Charis sat up on the cot, pulled her coverall into place Coverall? Something buried deep inside her questioned, and a seed of doubt plagued her. Yes, the post was very still. She went to the door, set her hands on either side of the sealed slit. Was she locked in? But when she applied pressure, the portal opened and she was able to look out into the corridor.

The doors along it gaped open as she slipped into freedom. Listening brought no trace of sound, no murmur of voices or the heavy breathing of a sleeper. She went on down the hall, the floor chill to her bare feet.

But this—all of this, whispered that rebellious voice deep within her, she had done before. Yet on the surface, this was the here and now. The rooms were empty; she paused at each to make sure of that. Then the fourth room: a com screen against its wall, chairs and piles of record tapes. The com—she could use its sweep, try to pick up the government base. But first she must make sure she was safely alone.

A hurried search of the post, room by room. Time—it was a matter of time. Then she was back in the com room, leaning over the key board, picking out the proper combination to trigger a sweep ray.

A wait, and then a signal to the northeast. The visa-plate clouded and then cleared. Charis dodged from her position before it. A man was standing out of the mist, a man wearing a dingy uniform of a trader. Charis studied him, but he was unknown to her. Only the illegal blaster holstered at his belt made him different from any other fringe crewman. Charis's hand swept out to break contact.

She activated the sweep once again, tried south, and picked a signal—the insignia of Survey with a seal of Embassy. Slowly then she began to click out a message for the tape.

She was on a hillside. It was cold, dark, and she was running, running until her breath made a sharp stab beneath her ribs. The hunt would be up soon. Or would Tolskegg be willing to let her go, to die alone in the heights of exhaustion, starvation, or at the claws of some beast? He had Demeter and the settlement below now within his hold.

Demeter! The part of her which had been denying that this *was* the here and now struggled. Charis shook with more than cold. She was climbing to the heights above the settlement, yet the belief that this was all false grew stronger and stronger.

A dream. And there were those who used dreams and the stuff of dreams as a potter spun clay on his wheel. If she was caught in a dream, then she must wake—wake soon. Not a dream. Yes—a dream. She felt her own exhaustion, the pinch of hunger which was pain, the rough ground over which she stumbled, the bushes she grasped to steady her.

Not real—a dream! The bushes thinned until they were unsubstantial ghosts of themselves. Through their wavering outlines she saw a wall—yes, wall, solid wall. She was not on Demeter—she was—she was . . .

Warlock! As if the recognition of that name were a key, the now shadowy slope of Demeter vanished, driven away like smoke by a rising wind. She lay on a pad of mats. To her right was a window giving on the dark of night with a frosting of stars in the sky. This was Warlock and the Citadel of the Wyverns.

She did not move but lay quietly trying to separate dream from reality. The post—it had been raided. That Survey officer Shann Lantee— She could see him as plainly now as if he stood before her, the blood-spattered alien spear held between them.

The spear. It had splintered under the action of the Wyvern. The broken bits had moved in that weird dance until they had fallen in a pattern which had awakened such rage in the Warlockians. And that rage . . .

Charis sat bolt upright on the mats. Lantee crumbling under the Power of the Wyverns, herself returned to relive portions of the past—for what purpose she could not divine. Why had that rage been turned on Lantee? In a way, it had been her fault for summoning Cytha. She had been too impulsive.

Her hands went to the pouch at her belt. It was empty of the disk. That had been in her hand when the Power had taken her on the shore. Had she dropped it or had they taken it from her?

That could mean that the Wyverns no longer considered her in the guise of friend or ally. What *had* the broken spear meant to them? Without the disk Charis was a prisoner here in this room. At least there was no reason why she could not attempt at once to find out what bonds had been set upon her freedom. Would she discover herself as unable to move as she had been on her flight along the shore when it had suited the Wyverns to control her?

"Tsstu?" Charis held that call to hardly above a whisper. She did not know how much of an ally the small curl-cat could be against the Wyverns, but she had come to depend upon her for companionship more heavily than she had guessed.

A drowsy sound came from the shadow directly below the window near which her head had rested. Tsstu lay there, curled in a ball, her eyes closed, her ears folded back tight against her head. Charis stooped and drew her fingers lightly across that head.

"Tsstu," she whispered coaxingly. Was the curl-cat— she had adopted Lantee's name for Tsstu's species since it fitted so well—deep in her own kind of dreaming, too deep to be aroused now?

The ears twitched and slits of eyes showed between lids. Then Tsstu yawned widely, her yellow tongue curled up and out. She lifted her head to eye Charis.

To communicate more than just vague impressions without the aid of the disk—could she do that? Charis made a sudden swoop to gather up the curl-cat, holding Tsstu aloft so that those narrow felinelike eyes looked straight into hers. Was Tsstu so closely linked to the Wyverns that she would serve them rather than Charis now?

Away, the girl thought, out of here.

"Rrrruuuu." That was agreement.

Tsstu wriggled vigorously in her grasp, wanting her freedom. Charis obeyed her wish. The curl-cat approached the doorway on pad-feet, elongating and flattening her body so that she had the appearance of a hunter on stalk. She stared into the corridor, her head raised a little, her ears spread to their widest. Charis guessed that every sense the curl-cat had was analyzing, scouting, for them. Tsstu glanced back at the girl, summoned—

This way led to the assembly rooms, to other private chambers such as hers, prepared for dreamers. Whether or not the corridor would eventually take them outside Charis did not know; she could only hope and rely upon Tsstu.

Even without the disk she strove to pick up any mind touch, any intimation that the Wyverns were about. Twice Charis was sure she had brushed beamed thoughts, not enough to read, just enough to be certain that they did exist. Otherwise, as in the trading post, she might be walking through a deserted dwelling.

Tsstu seemed confident of her path, trotting noiselessly along, choosing without hesitation whenever the corridor branched or was crossed by another passage. Charis was already out of the small portion of the maze that she knew. And she was conscious of the fact that the curl-cat had guided her into a section where the light from the walls was dimmer, the walls themselves rougher, narrower. She gained a feeling of age. Then the light was gone from the whole wall surface, lingering only in some places. Charis had to study closely before she saw the purpose of those remaining patches. They made out a design not unlike the whorls and circling on the disks. Here on the walls were some of the same symbols of power which the Wyverns had harnessed to their bidding.

But these patterns were not finished nor as crisp and cleanly cut as those on the disks. Larger, cruder, could they still open doorways for the initiated?

Tsstu continued with confidence. The even temperature of the other corridors failed. Charis put fingers to the nearest spiral and jerked them away as her flesh shrank from the heat there. She coughed, her throat dry. Where or what was this place?

In spite of an inner warning, she could not help but follow some of the designs with her eyes, looking ahead to pick them up, keeping them in sight until they were behind her. They blanketed her general field of vision until all she could see were the designs, and she halted with a cry of fear.

"Tsstu!"

Soft fur against her ankles, a reassurance in her mind. The curl-cat must not be affected by the same illusions as now imprisoned the girl. But to walk through this blackness where only the whorls, circles, lines had any existence for her was more than Charis could bring herself to do. Fear—overwhelming, panic-raising fear—

"Meeeerreee!"

Charis could feel Tsstu, she could hear her, but she could not see the curl-cat. She could see nothing but the patterns.

"Back!" her word was a hoarse whisper. Only now Charis was not sure where back was. To take a step could plunge her into unknown chaos.

There was one design out of that mass of patterns— somehow she was able to fasten on that. Larger, sprawled out in crude length where she was used to it in a compact, clearly defined circle—this was her own disk pattern. She was certain of that.

"Tsstu!" She caught up the curl-cat by touch. Only those lines of dull silver glowed in the darkness. Concentrate on this design as she had on the disk and so—escape?

Charis hesitated. Escape to where? Return to the raided post? To the moss meadow? She must have a strong visual picture of her goal or the transport would not occur. Post? Meadow? Neither was where she wanted to go now. It was not just escape she wanted, it was knowledge of what was happening and why. But one could not gain that so . . .

Then—she was there. Lines of Wyverns, all seated cross-legged on mats, all intent upon two in the center. Lines of Wyverns, circles of them, for the chamber was a bowl-shaped place made up of climbing ledges, circling a space.

In that space Gysmay and her shadow-patterned companion stood alone. They faced each other, those two, and between them on the dark of the floor were splinters, needlelike pieces of all colors of the rainbow. The two were intent upon those splinters as were all others in that chamber.

Charis's hair stirred with electricity, her skin prickled. There was such power here, loosed, flowing, that she reacted to it physically. None of those about her had noted her coming; they stared at the splinters, concentrating their power.

The splinters rose upon their points, whirled, danced, spun into the air to form a small cloud which first encircled Gysmay. Three times about her body, beginning at waist height, then at her throat, lastly about her head. Then they spun away to the open between the two Wyverns, came apart in a tinkling rain to form a design on the floor. And from those that watched there came to Charis a ripple of emotion, some decision or demand or bargaining point, she was not sure which, had been stated.

Again the needles rose in their point-dance, leaped into the air to form a cloud which now wreathed the shadowed Wyvern. And Charis thought that they spun more slowly this time and that the cloud did not glint with bright colors but was more subdued. It broke and tinkled down to deliver the answer, counterargument, disagreement—three in one.

And again there was to be sensed a wave of approbation from some of the watchers, but a weaker one. The company was divided upon some issue and their discussion conducted so Charis watched, supposing that Gysmay was about to answer, for the needles were rising again.

But this time their dance was less prolonged and the cloud they formed swayed neither to one of the Wyverns nor to the other. It was a tight saucer-shape rising higher and higher, straight up until it was level with the fourth and top tier of the ledges.

The company watched in shocked surprise. This they had not expected. Gysmay and her companions held their disks. But if they strove to call the needles, those were now out of their control. The cloud swayed back and forth as if it clung to some unseen pendulum. And each swing brought it closer to where Charis stood.

Suddenly it broke from that measured swing to dart at her. She cried out as it whirled about her head, swiftly, almost menacingly. The two nearest Wyverns were on their feet, while all below focused on the girl.

Twice, three times, the cloud wreathed her and then it was gone, out over the open, descending. But Charis could not move; the restraint of the power held her prisoner. The cloud broke, rained its substance down to the floor, but she could see no design, only a meaningless jumble.

At the same time she moved, not of her own volition, but under the will of those about her, descending from tier to tier until she stood in the open, equidistant from the two witches.

"What is read is read. To each dreamer, a dream as is the will of Those Who Have Dreamed Before. It would seem, Dreamer of Other World Dreams, that you, also, have a word in this matter—"

"In what matter?" Charis asked aloud.

"In the matter of life and death, of your blood and our blood, of past and future" was the evasive answer.

Where she found the words and the courage to say them in an even voice, Charis did not know as she replied: "If that is the answer, I have been granted—" she nodded at the fallen needles "—then you needs must read it for me, O, One of All Wisdom."

It was the shadow-laced Wyvern who answered: "But this is beyond our reading, though it *has* meaning since the Power moved its fashioning. We can only believe that its time is not yet. But time itself is an enemy in this matter. When one weaves a dream there must be no breaking of the thread of warp and woof. In our dreams, you and yours are unwelcome—"

"Those of my blood have died on the shore," Charis retorted. "Yet I cannot believe that it was by your hands and will—"

"No—by their own. For they began an ill dream and twisted the pattern. They have done a thing which is beyond straightening now." Gysmay was all anger, though that emotion was controlled and perhaps the more deadly because of that control. "They have given those who cannot dream another kind of power to break the long-laid design. Thus they must be hunted! They would overturn all reason and custom, and to that the end is slaying—and the slaying has already begun. We want no more of you. It shall be so." She clapped her hands and the needles jumped, collecting into a heap.

"Perhaps—" the shadowed Wyvern spoke.

"Perhaps?" echoed Charis. "Speak plainly to me now, Holder of Old Wisdom. I have seen a dead man of my race lying by a broken dwelling, and with him was a weapon which was not his. Yet among you I have seen no arms save the disks of Power. What evil walks this world? It is not of my making nor of the man Lantee's." She did not know why she added that, save that Lantee had had friendly contact with the witches.

"You are of one breed with the makers of this trouble!" Gysmay's thought was like a sharp hiss.

"The spear," Charis persisted, "this is of your kind, not mine! And a man died of it."

"Those who dream not—they hunt, they kill with such. And now they have broken the ancient law and run to do evil in the service of strangers. Those strangers have given them a protection against the Power so that they may not be brought back into order again. Perhaps this was not of your doing, for among us you have dreamed true and know the Power in its proper use. And the man Lantee, together with the one other who was with him from the earlier time, he, too, has dreamed—though that was out of all custom. But now come those who do not dream, to uphold the evil of not-dreaming. And our world will fall apart unless we hasten to the mending."

"But still," the shadowed Wyvern's quieter message came, "there is the pattern we cannot read and which we may not push away unheeded, for it was born of what we evoked here to answer us in our need. Therefore, there is a use for you, though we know not yet what it may be, nor do you. This you must learn for yourself and bring to aid the greater design—"

There was no mistaking the warning lying in that. Charis could only guess at the meaning behind the circumlocution of speech. An off-world party—probably the Jacks who had raided the post—had freed some of the males from the control of the Wyvern matriarchs. And these were now fighting for or with the strangers. In return, the Wyverns seemed about to organize some counterblow against all off-worlders.

"This great design—is it being readied against those of my blood?" Charis asked.

"I m

"It must be carefully woven, then aimed and dreamed." Again only half an answer. "But it will break your pattern as you have broken ours."

"And I have a part in this?"

"You have received an answer which we could not read. Discover its meaning and maybe it will be for us also."

"She breaks our pattern here," Gysmay interrupted. "Send her into the Place Without Dreams that she may not continue to disrupt what we do here!"

"Not so! She was answered; she has a right to learn the meaning of that answer. Send her forth from this place, yes—that we shall do. But into the Darkness Which Is Naught? No—that is against her rights. Time grows short, Dreamer. Dream true if you would save the breaking of your pattern Now—get you hence!"

The tiered chamber, the watching Wyverns, vanished. Night was dark about Charis, but she could hear the murmur of sea waves not too far away. She breathed fresh air and above her were stars. Was she back on shore?

No. As her eyes adjusted to the very dim light, she was able to see that she stood on a high point of rock; around her on all sides was the wash of waves. She must be marooned on a rocky spear in what might be the middle of the ocean.

Afraid to take a step in any direction, Charis dropped down to her knees, hardly believing this could be true. Tsstu stirred, made a small questioning sound, and Charis's breath caught in a half-sob of incredulous protest.

X

"THE DREAM is yours. Dream true."

Rock, an islet of bare rock, high above the sea with no path down its steep walls against which waves thundered. Overhead the cries of birds disturbed from their nesting holes by her coming. In the half-light of early morning Charis surveyed her perch. The first bewilderment of her arrival was gone, but her uneasiness now had a base of fear.

There was a series of sharp, shallow ledges leading down from the point of rock where she crouched to a wider open space sheltered on one side by a ridge. Some vegetation, pallid and sickly looking, straggled in that pocket of earth. She rose to look out over the sea, having no idea where she was now in relation to the Citadel or the main continent.

Some distance away there was another blot which must mark a second rock island, but it was too far to make out clearly. The finality which had been in her dismissal from the Wyvern assemblage clung. They had sent her here, and she could only believe that they would do nothing to get her back. Her escape must be of her own devising.

"Meeerrreee?" Tsstu squatted on the rock, her whole stance expressing her dislike of these surroundings.

"Where do we go?" Charis asked. "You know as much as I."

The curl-cat looked at her through eyes slitted against the force of the rising wind. Charis shivered. There was a promise of rain in the feel of that breeze, she thought. To be caught on this barren rock in a storm . . .

Only that half-pocket below offered any shelter at all; best get into it now. Tsstu was prudently already on the way, though with caution as she clawed along the ledges.

Rain sure enough, great drops slapping down. But rain meant water to drink. Charis welcomed those runnels which spattered into the pockets of rock. With the gift of rain water, this storm could be a blessing for them both.

The birds which had cried overhead were now gone. Tsstu, prowling their scrap of ground, went to work at a matted tangle against the ridge wall. She looked up with a trickle of white coursing over her chin, which she swept away with a swift swipe of tongue.

"—ree—" She pushed her head back into the tangle and then backed out, coming to Charis carrying something in her mouth with delicate care. When the girl put out her hand, Tsstu dropped into it a ball which could only be an egg.

Hunger fought with distaste and won. Charis broke a small hole in the top of that sphere and sucked its contents, trying not to notice the taste. Eggs and rain water — How long would they last? How long would the two of them last perched up here, especially if the wind grew strong enough to lick them off?

"The dream is yours. Dream true." Could this be only

one of those very real dreams which the Wyverns were able to evoke? Charis could not remember that in any of those visions she had felt the need to eat or drink. Dream or real? Charis had no evidence either way.

But there had to be some way of escape!

The ridge at her back kept a measure of the rain from them, but the water gathering on the higher level drained down into this slight basin, pooling up about the roots of the few small plants. The earth about them grew slick.

If she only had the disk! But she had not had that back in that passage where the patterns had glowed on the walls. Yet her concentration upon those designs had taken her into the Wyvern assembly.

Suppose she had the same means of leaving here— where would she go? Not back to the Citadel; that was enemy territory now. To the raided post? No, unless she was only seeking a hiding place. But that was not what she wanted.

Wyvern witches against off-worlders. If the natives moved only against the Jacks and their own renegade males, that was none of her battle. But they were seeing *all* off-worlders as enemies now. If this rock exile was merely a device to keep her out of battle, it was a well-planned one. But she was of one stock; the Wyverns, no matter how much they had been in accord, were alien. And when it came to drawing battle lines, she was on the other side, whether her original sympathies lay there or not.

No, Charis did not care what happened to the scum which had turned Jack here; the quicker they were dealt with the better. But they should be disciplined by their own kind.

Lantee and this Ragnar Thorvald who represented off-world law on Warlock and who now were apparently lumped with those to be finished off, Wyvern-fashion—they must have a say. If they could be warned, then there might still be time to summon the Patrol to handle the Jacks and prove to the Wyverns that all off-worlders were *not* alike.

A warning. But even with the disk Charis could not reach the government base. You had to have a previous memory of any point, be able to picture it in your mind, in order to use the Power to reach it. And Lantee—what had happened to him at the post? Was he even still alive after that mind blast from the Wyverns?

Could—just possibly—could you use a *person* as a journey goal? Not to summon him to you as she had so disastrously done with Gytha at the post, but to go to him? It was action she had never tried. But it was a thought.

Only first—the means. With a disk, one focused on the pattern until one's eyes were set, and one's concentration reached the necessary pitch to use one's will as a springboard into Otherwhere, or through it into another place.

Back in the passage, she had involuntarily used the glowing design on the wall to project her into the Wyvern council, though then she had not controlled her place of arrival.

What was important then was not the disk itself but the design it bore. Suppose she could reproduce that pattern here, concentrate upon it. Escape? It might be her one chance. Manifestly she had no means of leaving here otherwise. So why not try the illogical?

Then—go where? The post? The moss meadow? Any point on which she could fix an entrance would bring her no closer to the base of the Survey men. But if she could join Lantee—Him she could visualize strongly

105

enough to use. The only other possibility was Jagan and she could not obtain any aid from the trader, even if he were still alive.

To join Lantee who, by his own account, had some experience with Wyvern dreaming and Power—might that not make him more receptive as a focal point? There was so much she had to guess about this, but it was the best chance she could see now. *If* she could set up the liberating pattern at all.

What were her means? The rock was too rough to serve as a surface on which to scratch lines. The slick clay at the edge of the growing pool caught Charis's attention. It was a relatively flat stretch and one could make an impression on it with a sharp stone or a branch from one of the bushes. But she had to do it right.

Charis closed her eyes and tried to build within her mind the all-important memory. There was a wavy line which curled back upon its length—so. Then the break which came—thus. Something else—something missing. Her agitation grew as she strove to fit in the part she could not remember. Maybe if she drew it out she would . . .

But the expanse of the clay was now too well covered by the pool water. And the wind was rising. With Tsstu curled close against her, Charis hugged the protecting ridge rock. There was nothing to do until the storm died.

Within a very short time Charis began to fear that they would not survive the fury of the wind, the choking drive of the rain. Only the fact that the ridge wall was there and they were tight against it gave them anchorage. The downpour continued to raise the pool until the water lapped Charis's cold feet and legs, but then it reached new runnels to feed it to the sea below.

Tsstu was a source of warmth in her arms and the

curl-cat's vague communication was a reassurance, too. A confidence flowed from the animal to the girl, not steadily, but when she needed it most. Charis wondered just how much of what had happened to them Tsstu understood. Their band of mind-touch was so narrow the girl could not judge the intelligence of the Warlockian animal by the forms of comparison she knew. Tsstu might be far more than she seemed or be assessed as less because of the lack of full communication.

There came a time when the wind no longer lashed at their refuge or poked in finger-gusts to try to loosen their hold. The sky lightened and the rain, from a blustering wall of driven water, slackened into a drizzle. Still Charis was not sure of the design. But she watched the shore of the pool avidly, wondering whether she could bare the clay by cupping out water with her hands.

The sky was streaked with gold when she edged forward and twisted a length of water-soaked frond from one of the bushes. To strip away leaves and give herself a writing point was no problem. Impatience possessed her now—she *must* try this slender hope.

She cupped out some of the pool water by hand, clearing a stretch of smooth blue clay. Now! Charis found her fingers shaking a little; she set her will and muscle power to control that trembling as she put the point of her writing tool in the sticky surface.

Thus—the wavy line which was the base of the design to her thinking. Yes! Now for the sharp counter-stroke to bisect it at just the proper angle. There—correct. But the missing part . . .

Charis shut her eyes tightly. Wave, line— What *was* the other? Useless. She could not remember.

Bleakly she looked down at the almost complete pattern. But "almost" would not serve; it had to be perfect. Tsstu sat beside her, staring with feline intensity at the marks in the clay. Suddenly she shot out a paw, planted it flat before Charis could interfere. At the girl's cry, the curl-cat's ears folded and she growled softly, but she withdrew her forefoot, leaving the impress of three pads set boldly in the mud.

Three indentations? no—two! Charis laughed. Tsstu's memory was the better. She rubbed the mud clear, began to draw again—this time far more swiftly—with self-confidence. Wavy line, cut, two ovals—not quite where Tsstu had placed them, but here and here.

"Meeerrreee!"

"Yes!" Charis echoed that cry of triumph. "Will it work, little one? Will it work? And where do we go?"

But she knew she had already made up her mind as to that. Not a place but a *man* was her goal—at least at first try. If she could not join Lantee, they would try for the moss meadow and the chance of working their way south to the base from there. But that meant a waste of time they might not have to spend. No—for what might be the safety of all their kind on this world, Lantee was her first goal.

First she began to build her mental picture of the Survey officer, fitting in every small detail that memory supplied, and she found there were more of those to summon than she had believed. His hair, black, crisply curling like Tsstu's; his brown face sober and masked until he smiled but then softening about his mouth and eyes; his spare, wiry body in the green-brown uniform of his corps; his tall boots of copper; rubbing against those, his companion Taggi. Erase the wolverine, a second living thing might confuse the Power.

Charis found that she could not divide the two in her

mind-picture. Man and animal, they clung together despite her efforts to forget Taggi and see only Lantee. Once more she built up the picture of Shann Lantee as she had seen him at the post before she had summoned Gytha. Just so he had stood, looked, been. Now!

Tsstu had come back into her arms, her claws caught in Charis's already slitted tunic. Charis regarded the curl-cat with a smile.

"We had better finish this flitting about soon or you will have me reduced to rags. Shall we try it?"

"—reee—" Agreement by mind-touch, eager anticipation. Tsstu appeared to have no doubts that they would go somewhere.

Charis stared down at the pattern.

Cold—no light at all—a terrible emptiness. Life was not. She wanted to scream under a torture which was not of body but of mind. Lantee—where *was* Lantee? Dead? Was this death into which she had followed him?

Cold again—but another kind of cold. Light—light which carried the promise of life she knew and understood. Charis fought down the churning sickness which had come from that terror of the place where life did not exist.

A rank smell, a growling answered by Tsstu's "rrruu-ugh" of warning. Charis saw the rocky waste about them and—the brown Taggi. The wolverine lumbered back and forth, pausing now and then to snarl. And Charis caught the feeling of fear and bewilderment which moved him. Always his pacing brought him back to the figure which squatted in a small fissure, huddling there, facing outward.

"Lantee!" Charis's cry of recognition was almost a paean of thanksgiving. Her gamble had paid off; they had reached the Survey man.

But if he heard her, saw her, he made no response. Only Taggi turned and came to her at an awkward run, his round head up, his harsh cry sounding not in warning-off anger but as a petition for aid. Lantee must be hurt. Charis ran.

"Lantee?" she called again as she went to her knees before the crevice into which he had crawled. Then she saw his face clearly.

At their first meeting his expression had been guarded, remote, but it had been—alive. This man breathed; she could see the rise and fall of his chest. His skin—she reached out her hand, rested finger tips briefly on his wrist, then raised them to his cheek—his skin was neither burning with fever nor unduly chill. Only what had made him truly a man and not a living husk was gone, sucked or driven out of him. By that bolt of the Wyvern's wrath?

Charis sat back on her heels and looked about. This was not the clearing before the post, so he had not remained where she had seen him fall. She could hear the sea. They were somewhere in the wilds along the coast. How and why he had come here did not matter now.

"Lantee—Shann—" She made a coaxing sound of his name as one might to attract the attention of a child. There was no flicker of response in his dead eyes, on the husk of a face.

The wolverine pushed against her, his rank odor strong. Taggi's head moved, his jaws opened and closed on her hand, not in anger but as a bid for attention. Seeing that he had that, Taggi released his hold, swung around facing inland, his growl a plain warning of danger in that direction.

Tsstu's ears, which had flattened at first sight of the Terran animal, spread again. She clawed at Charis.

Something was coming; her own warning was piercingly sharp—they *must* go.

Charis reached again for Lantee's wrist, her fingers closed firmly as she pulled him forward. Whether she could get him moving she did not know.

"Come—come, we must go." Perhaps her words had no meaning, but he *was* responding to her tug, crawling out of the crevice, rising to his feet as she stood up and drew him with her. He would keep moving as long as she kept hold of his arm, Charis discovered, but if she broke contact, he stopped.

So propelling him, the girl turned south, Tsstu prowling ahead, Taggi forming a rear guard. Who or what could be behind them she did not know; her worst suspicions said Jack. Lantee wore no weapon, not even a stunner. And thrown stones were no protection against blasters. To find a refuge in which to hole up was perhaps their only hope if they were trailed.

Luckily, the terrain before them was not too rough. She could not have hauled Lantee, even docile as he was, up or down climbs. Not too far ahead were signs of broken country, an uneven line of outcrops sharp against the sky. And somewhere among those they might find a temporary sanctuary. Taggi had disappeared. Twice Charis had turned to watch for the wolverine, not daring to call. She remembered the whistle she had heard back in the moss meadow when she had first sighted the Survey officer and his four-footed companion. That summons she could not duplicate.

Now she hurried on. Under her urging, Lantee lengthened his stride, but there was no sign that he was responding to anything but her pull on his arm. He might have been a robot. Any warning she had would mean nothing to him in his present condition, and whether that had been caused only by temporary shock from the encounter with the blast of Wyvern power or something more lasting, she could not tell.

It would not be long until sunset, Charis knew. To reach the broken land before the failing of the light was her purpose. And she made it. Tsstu scouted out what they needed, a ledge forming a good overhang which was half cave. Charis pushed Lantee ahead of her into that growing pool of shadow and pulled him down. He sat there, staring unseeingly out into the twilight.

Emergency rations? His uniform belt had a series of pockets in its broad length and Charis set about searching them. A message or record tape in the first, then a packet of small tools for which she could not imagine any use apart from complicated installation repairs, three credit tokens, a case for identity and permit cards containing four she did not pause to read, another packet of simple first-aid materials—perhaps more to the purpose now than the rest. She worked from right to left, emptying each pocket and then restoring its contents, while Lantee paid no heed to her search. Now—this was what she had hoped for. She had seen just such tubes carried by the ranger on Demeter. Sustain tablets. Not only would they allay hunger, but they added a booster which restored and nourished nervous energy.

Four of them. Two Charis dropped back into the tube which she placed in her own belt pouch. One she mouthed and chewed with vigor. There was no taste at all, but she got it down. The other she held uncertainly. How could she get it into Lantee? She doubted if he would eat in his present condition. She would have to see if a certain amount of absorption would come by the only way left. She gathered two pebbles from the ground and brushed them back and forth on her ragged tunic to clean them from dust as well as she could, next, that identity card case, also dusted for surface dirt. With the rubbing of the tablet between the two pebbles, Charis obtained a powder, caught on the slick surface of the case.

Then, forcing his mouth open, the girl was able to brush that powder into Lantee's mouth. It was the best she could do. And just maybe the reviving powers of the highly concentrated Sustain might cut down the effects of the shock—or whatever affected him now.

XI

WHILE SHE still had light, Charis set about making their half-cave into more of a fortress, pushing and carrying loose stones to build up a low wall across its front. If they kept well down behind that, the green of her tunic and the green-brown of Lantee's uniform would not be too noticeable. She bit at a ragged nail as she crawled back under cover.

The pocket of shadow had deepened and Charis put out a questioning hand to guide her. She touched Lantee's shoulder and moved, to huddle down close beside him. Tsstu flitted in, "meeerreeed" once, and then left on a hunt of her own. Of Taggi, there had been no sign since they had come into the broken land. Perhaps the wolverine, too, had gone in quest of food.

Charis let her head fall forward to rest on her knees. In this cramped space it was necessary to ball one's body into the smallest possible compass. She was not really tired; the Sustain tablet was working. But she needed to think. The Wyverns had warned her that time was against her. She had won free from the sea-rock to which they had exiled her, but perhaps she had made the wrong choice of escape. In his present condition, Lantee was no ally but a responsibility. With the coming of light she could redraw the pattern, get as far south as the moss meadow. How much farther beyond that lay the government base she had no idea. But if she kept on following the shore she would eventually reach it.

But—Lantee? She could not take him with her, she was sure of that. And to leave him here in his condition —Charis shied from that solution every time the brutal necessity for action presented it. He was no friend; they had no acquaintance past that one meeting by the post. He had no claim on her at all and the need for action was urgent.

There were times when one human life was expendable for the whole. But, well as she knew the bitter logic of that reasoning, Charis found a barrier in her against her following it as high and firm as the barriers which the Wyverns had used to control her. Well, she could do nothing during the hours of dark. Maybe before morning Lantee would come out of it, out of this state of nonbeing. It was childish to cling to such hope but she did. Now she tried to will herself to sleep, a sleep past the entry of any dream.

"—ah—ahhhhhhh—"

The plaint was that of pain. Charis strove to deafen herself against it.

"—ah—ahhhhhhh!"

The girl's head came up. There was a stirring beside her. She could not see Lantee save as a dim bulk in the gloom, but her hand went out to feel the convulsive shudders which tore him. And always came that small thread of a moan which must mark some unendurable agony.

"Lantee!" She shook his arm and he fell over against her, his head now resting on her knee, so that the shivering which rocked him became partly hers. His moaning had stopped, but his breath came and went in great sucking gasps, as if he could not get oxygen enough to satisfy the needs of his trembling body.

"Shann—what is it?" Charis longed for light enough to see his face. When she had nursed those struck down by the white plague on Demeter, she had known this same sick fear, this same courage sapping frustration. What could she do, what could anyone do? She drew him toward her so that his head rested in her lap, tried to hold him still. But just as he had been apathetic and robot-like before, so now he was restless. His head turned back and forth as that horrible gasping racked him.

"Rrrruuuu." Out of nowhere Tsstu came, a shadow. The curl-cat was on Lantee's chest, crouched low, clinging with claws when Charis tried to push her away. Then a growl and Taggi burst around the stones Charis had set up, came to nuzzle against Lantee's twisted body as if, with Tsstu, he strove to hold the sufferer still. Need—it was a cloud about the four of them—the blind call for help which Lantee did not have to put into words for Charis to feel, the concern of the animals, her own helplessness. This was a crisis point, she realized that. The Survey man was fighting a battle, and if he lost—?

"What can I do?" she cried aloud. This was not an affair of the body—she had delved deeply enough into the Wyvern Power to know that—but of mind, of—of identity.

Will—that was the springboard of Wyvern power.

They willed what they wished, and it *was!* She was willing now—willing Lantee to . . .

Dark and cold and that which was nothing once again, this was the space into which her desire to help was drawing her, a space which was utterly alien to her kind. Dark—cold. But now— Two small lights, flickering, then growing stronger, though the dark and cold fought to extinguish them; two lights which drew closer to her and grew and grew. She did not reach out her hands to take up those lights, but they came as if she had called. And then Charis was aware that there was a third light, and *she* furnished the energy on which it fed.

Three lights joined to speed through that dark in search. No thought, no speech among them; just the compulsion to answer a calling need. For the dark and cold were all-encompassing, a sea of black having no shore, no islands.

Island? Faint, *so* faint, a glimmer showed on the sea. They spun together, those three lights, and struck down to the small spark gleaming in that encroaching and swallowing dark. Now there was a fourth light like an ash-encrusted coal in a near-dead fire. Together the three aimed at that fire, but there was no touching it: They had not the power to strike through, and the fire was near extinction.

Then the light which was fed by Charis's energy and will soared, drawing also that which was the animals. She reached out, not with a physical arm or hand but with an extension of her inner force, and touched one of her companion lights.

It snapped toward her. She was rent, to writhe in pain as emotions which were alien warred against that which was Charis alone—wild, raw emotions which boiled and frothed, which dashed her in and about. But she fought back, strove to master and won to an uneasy stability. And then she reached out again and drew to her the second spark.

Once again she was in tumult, and even greater was the fight she had to wage for supremacy. But the urgency which had drawn all three, the need to go to the dying fire, laid upon them now the need for acting as one. And when Charis called upon that need, they obeyed.

Down to that glimmer which was now far spent sped a bolt of flaming force raised to the highest possible pitch. That broke through, pierced to the heart of the fire.

Turmoil for a space. Then it was as if Charis raced wildly down a corridor into which emptied many doors. From behind each of these came people and things she did not know, who grasped at her, tried to shout messages in her ears, impress upon her their importance, until Charis was deafened, driven close to the edge of sanity. To that corridor she could see no end.

The voices screamed, but through them came other sounds—a growling, a squalling—equal to the voices, demanding attention in their turn. Charis could not run much farther . . .

Silence, abrupt, complete—and in its way terrifying, too. Then—light. And she had a body again. Aware first of that, Charis ran a hand down that body in wonder and thankfulness. She looked about her. Under her sandaled feet was sand, silver sand. But this was not the shore of the sea. In fact, vision in any direction was not clear, for there was a mist which moved in spirals and billows, a mist of green, the same green as the tunic she wore.

The mist curled, writhed, held a darker core. She saw movement in that core, as if an arm had drawn aside a curtain.

"Lantee!"

He stood there, facing her. But it was no longer the shell of a man she saw. There was life and awareness back in his body and mind. He held out his hand to her.

"Dream . . . ?"

Was it all a dream? She had known such clarity of vision before in the dream Otherwhere of the Wyverns.

"I don't know," she answered his half-question.

"You came—*you!*" There was a kind of wondering recognition in his voice which she understood. They had been together in that place where their kind was not. The four fires, joined together, had now broken the bonds which had held him in a place their species should never know.

"Yes." Lantee nodded even though Charis had put none of that into words. "You and Taggi and Tsstu. Together you came, and together we broke out."

'But this?" Charis gazed about at the green mist. "Where is *this?*"

"The Cavern of the Veil—of illusions. But this I believe *is* a dream. Still they strive to keep us that much in bonds."

"For dreams there are answers." Charis went down on her knees and smoothed the sand. With one finger tip she traced her design. It was not clear in the podery stuff, but there was enough, she hoped, to serve her purpose. Then she looked at Lantee.

"Come." Charis held out her hand. "Think of a half-cave—" swiftly she described the place they had been in at night "—and keep hold. We must try to return."

She felt his grip tense and harden, his stronger fingers cramping hers until her flesh numbed. And then she centered all of her mind on the picture of the ledge cave and the pattern. . . .

Charis was stiff and cold, her arm ached, her hand was numb. Behind her was a rock wall, over her head an extension of it, and from before her a breath of sun heat. There was a sigh and she glanced down.

Lantee lay there, curled up awkwardly, his head in her lap, his hand clutching hers in that numbing grip. His face was drawn and haggard, as if he had aged planet years since she had seen him last. But the slack blankness which had been so terrifying was gone. He stirred and opened his eyes, first bewildered, but then knowing, recognizing her.

He raised his head.

"Dream!"

"Maybe. But we are back—here." Charis freed her hand from his hold and spread her cramped fingers. With her other hand she patted the nearest stone in her improvised wall to assure herself of its reality.

Lantee sat up and rubbed his hand across his eyes. But Charis remembered.

"Tsstu! Taggi!"

There was no sign of either animal. A small nagging fear began to nibble at her mind. They—*they* were those other lights. And she had lost them; they had not been in the place of green mist. Were they lost forever?

Lantee stirred. "They were with you—there?" It was not a question but a statement. He crawled out from under the ledge, whistled a clear rising note or two. Then he stooped and held out his hand again to draw her up beside him.

"Tsstu!" aloud she called the curl-cat.

Faint—very faint—an answer! Tsstu had not been abandoned in that place. But where was she?

"Taggi is alive!" Lantee's smile was real. "And he an-

119

swered me. It was different, that answer, from what it has ever been before, more as if we spoke."

"To have been *there*—might not that bring a change in us all?"

For a moment he was silent and then he nodded. "You mean because we were all one for a space? Yes, perhaps that cannot be ever put aside."

She had a spinning vision of that race down the endless corridor with its opening doors and the shouting figures emerging from them. Had those represented Lantee's memories, Lantee's thoughts? Not again did she want to face that!

"No," he agreed without need of speech from her, "not again. But there was then the need—"

"More than one kind of need." Charis shied away from any more mention of that mingling. "There's more trouble than Wyvern dreaming for us to consider now." She told him of what she had learned.

Lantee's mouth thinned into a straight line, his jaw thrust forward a little. "Thorvald was with them or at least at the Citadel when we found that spear. They may have put him away as they did me. Now they can move against all off-worlders without interference. We have a com-tech at the base, and a Patrol scout may have set down since I left—one was almost due. If that ship had not come in, Thorvald would have recalled me when he left. Two, maybe three, men were there and none of them armored against Wyvern control. We've been very cautious about trying to expand the base because we did want to maintain good relations. These Jacks have blown the whole plan! You say they have some Wyvern warriors helping them? I wonder how they worked that. From all we've been able to learn, and that's very little, the witches have a firm control over their males. That has always been one of the problems; makes it almost impossible for them to conceive of co-operation with us."

"The Jacks must have something to nullify the Power," Charis commented.

"That's all we need," he said bitterly. "But if they can nullify the Power, then how can the witches go up against them?"

"The Wyverns seem very sure of themselves." Charis had her own first doubts. With the assembly arrayed against her back at the Citadel, she had accepted their warning; her respect for their Power had not been shaken until this moment. But Lantee was right. If the invaders were able to nullify the Power to the extent of releasing the males who had always been under domination, then could the witches hope to battle the strangers themselves?

"No," Lantee continued, "they're very sure of themselves because they've never before come up against anything which threatened their hold on their people and their way of life. Perhaps they can't even conceive of the Power's being broken. We had hoped to make them understand eventually that there *were* other kinds of power, but we have not had time. To them this is a threat, right enough, but not *the* supreme threat I believe it is."

"Their Power *has* been broken," Charis said quietly.

"With a nullifier, yes. How soon do you suppose the truth of that will get through to them?"

"But we did not need this machine or whatever the Jacks have. We broke it—the four of us!"

Lantee stared at her. Then he threw back his head and laughed, not loudly but with the ring of real amusement.

"You are right. And what will our witches say to this, I wonder? Or do they already know? Yes, you freed me from whatever prison they consigned me to. And it *was* a prison!" His smile vanished, the drawn lines in his face sharpened. "So—their Power *can* be broken or circumvented in more ways than one. But I do not think that even that information will deter them from making the first move. And they must be stopped." He hesitated and then added in a rush of words, "I am not arguing that they should take the interference of the Jacks and not fight back. By their way of thinking their way of life is threatened. But if these witches go ahead as they plan and try to wipe us all off Warlock, supposing they *are* able to fight the Jack weapon or weapons, then they will have written the end to their own story themselves.

"For if this band of Jacks has come up with a nullifier to defeat the Power, others can, too. It will just be a matter of time until the Wyverns are under off-world control. And that mustn't happen!"

"You say that?" Charis asked curiously. "*You?*"

"Does that surprise you? Yes, they have worked on me and this was not the first time. But I, too, have shared their dreaming. And because I did and Thorvald did, we were that much closer to bridging the gap between us. We must be changed in part when we are touched by the Power. But though they may have to bend to weather a new wind—which will be very hard for them—they must not be swept away. Now—" he looked about him as if he could summon a copter out of the air "—we have to be on the move."

"I don't think they will allow us to return to the Citadel," Charis demurred.

"No, if they are working up to some stroke against off-worlders, they will have all the screens up about their prime base. Our own headquarters is the only place. From there we can signal for help. And if time is good to us, we can handle the Jacks before they do. But where we are now and how far from the base—" Lantee shook his head.

"Do you have your disk?" he added a moment later.

"No. But I don't need it." Just how true that was, Charis could not be sure. She had won off the rock island and out of the place of green mist without it, however. "But I've never seen your base."

"If I described it, as you did this rock hole for me, would that serve?"

"I don't know. The cavern was a dream, I think."

"And our bodies remained here as anchors to draw us back? That could well be. But there's no harm in trying."

The hour must have been close to midday; the sun was burning hot on the baked section of rock. And, as Lantee had pointed out, they were lost as far as landmarks were concerned. His suggestion was as good as any. Charis looked about for a patch of earth and a stone or stick to scratch with. But there was neither.

"I must have something which will make a mark."

"A mark?" Lantee echoed as he, too, surveyed their general surroundings. Then he gave an exclamation and snapped open a belt pocket to bring out the small aid kit. From its contents he selected a slender pencil which Charis recognized as sterile paint, made to cleanse and heal small wounds. It was of a greasy consistency. She tried it on the rock. The mark was faint but she could see it.

"Now," Lantee sat on his heels beside her, "we'll aim for a place I know about a half mile from the base."

"Why not the base itself?"

"Because there may be a reception waiting there that we wouldn't care to meet. I want to do some scouting before I walk into what might be real trouble."

He was right, of course. Either the Wyverns might already have made their move—for how could Charis guess how much time had actually passed since she had been wafted from the assembly to the island—or the Jacks, learning the undermanned status of the only legal hold on Warlock, had taken it over to save themselves from off-world interference.

"Right here—there's a lake shaped so." Lantee had taken the sterile stick from her and was drawing. "Then trees, a line of them standing this way. The rest is meadow land. We should be at this end of the lake."

It was hard to translate those marks into a real picture and Charis began to shake her head. Suddenly her companion leaned forward and laid his palms flat against her forehead just above her eyes.

XII

WHAT CHARIS saw was indistinct and fuzzy, not as clean-cut as a picture she recalled from her own memory, but perhaps enough for concentration. Only, with that fogged picture came other things; that corridor with the doors was beginning to take form behind the wood and lake. Charis struck Lantee's hand away and stared at him, breathing hard, trying to read an answering awareness in his eyes.

"We'll have to remember the dangers of that." Lantee spoke first.

"Not again! *Never* again!" Charis heard her voice grow shrill.

But already he was nodding in reply. "No, not again. But did you see enough of the other?"

"I hope so." She took the stick from him and chose a flat rock surface on which to sketch the Power design. It was when she was putting in the ovals Tsstu had remembered for her that Charis paused.

"Tsstu! I cannot leave her behind. And Taggi—"

She closed her eyes and sent out that silent call. "Tsstu, come! Come now!"

Touch! There came an overlapping of thought waves as fuzzy as the picture Lantee had beamed to her. And —refusal! Decided refusal—an abrupt breaking of contact. Why?

"There is no use," she heard Lantee say as she opened her eyes again.

"You reached Taggi." It was not a question.

"I reached him in a different way than I ever have before. He would not listen. He was occupied—"

"Occupied?" Charis wondered at his word choice. "Hunting?"

"I don't think so. He was exploring, trying something new which interested him so greatly he would not come."

"But they are *here*, back with us, not in Otherwhere?" Her relief was threatened by that recurring fear.

"I don't know where they are. But Taggi has no fear; he is only curious, very curious. And Tsstu?"

"She broke contact. But—yes—I think she had no fear either."

"We shall have to leave now!" Lantee continued.

If they could, Charis amended silently. She took his hand once more. "Think of your lake," she ordered and concentrated on the faint pattern on the rock.

Cool breeze—the murmur of it through leaves. The direct baking of the sun had been modified by a weaving of branches, and just before her was the shimmer of lake surface.

"We made it!" The tight grasp on her hand was gone. Lantee surveyed the site with a wary measuring, his nostrils slightly dilated as if, like Taggi, he could pick up and classify some alien scent.

There was a path along the lake shore, defined well enough to be clearly visible. Otherwise the place was as deserted as if no off-worlder had ever been there before.

"This way!" Lantee motioned her south, away from the thread of path. His voice was close to a whisper, as if he suspected they were scouting enemy-held territory. "There's a hill in this direction and from it we can get a good look at the base."

"But why—?" Charis began and was favored with an impatient frown from her companion.

"If there's any move being made, either by the Jacks or the witches, the first strike will be at the base. With Thorvald and me out of the way, the witches may be able to put Hantin, or any other off-worlder, right under control. And the Jacks could overrun the whole place easily, make a surprise attack and write off the base just as they wrote off the trading post."

She followed him with no more questions. On Demeter Charis had gone exploring with the ranger; she thought she knew a measure of woodcraft. But Lantee was as much at home in this business as Taggi could be. He slipped soundlessly from one piece of cover to another. However, she noted with some surprise, he did not display any outward signs of impatience when her clumsiness slowed them. And she was even a little resentful of what she came to believe was his forbearance.

Hot and very thirsty, Charis wriggled up a slope Lantee had led them to. She had a swelling bite delivered by the rightful inhabitant of an earthen run she had inadvertently crushed, and her throat ached with desert dryness before they lay side by side behind a screen of brush at the top of that rise.

A cluster of four bubble domes lay below and, farther away, a landing field. There was a light copter standing to one side of that, and on the rocket-blasted middle section stood a small spacer—a Patrol scout, Charis believed.

It was very peaceful there below. No one moved about the buildings, but pale flowers native to Warlock grew in the open space. And some brighter spots in those beds suggested that perhaps some off-world plants had been imported as an experiment.

"It looks all right—" she began.

"It looks all wrong!" His whisper carried something of the hiss of Wyvern anger.

There were no blast holes in the fabric of the domes as there had been at the raided post, nothing in sight which suggested trouble. But Lantee's concern was plain to read, and she returned to a second and more searching survey of the scene.

It must be midafternoon and there was a quality of drowsy peace down there. The inhabitants could all be dozing out the hours at their ease. Charis made up her mind not to ask for enlightenment but wait for her companion to volunteer the cause for his suspicion.

He began to talk softly, perhaps more as a listing of his own causes for suspicion aloud rather than as a sharing of information with Charis.

"Com mast down. Hantin's not out in the garden working on that new crossing bed of his. And Togi—Togi and the cubs—"

"Togi?" Charis dared to ask.

"Taggi's mate. She has two cubs and they spend every afternoon that's sunny down among those rocks. They're very fond of earth-wasp grubs and there's several colonies of them to be found there. Togi's been teaching the cubs how to dig them out."

But how could he be sure that just because a wolverine and her cubs were not at a certain place there was trouble below? Then Charis added that to the two other facts he had noted—the com mast down and that he had not seen one of the base personnel outside. But both of those were such little things—

"Put those three things together"—Lantee was either able to read her thoughts in part or was following her own line of reasoning with surprising accuracy—"and you have a wrong answer. On a base you come to follow habit. We have the com mast up always. That's orders and you don't change regulations unless there's an emergency. Hantin is experimenting with the crossing of some of the native plants with off-world varieties. He's hybrid-mad and he spends all his free time in the garden. And Togi is earth-wasp minded; only caging would keep her away from those rocks. And since we've yet to find any cage she can't break out of—" He looked glum.

"So—what do we do now?"

"We wait until dark. If the base is deserted and the com not wrecked—both of which are slim changes—there may be an opportunity to get a call off planet. But there's no use in trying to get down there now. Any approach would have to be made across the open."

He was right in that. The usual clearing about buildings ordered by custom in a frontier world was not as open here as it had been about Jagan's post. But there was no brush or trees or other cover growth left within a good distance of any of the four domes or the landing field. To approach those meant advancing in the open.

Lantee rolled over on his back and lay staring up into the bush they were using as a screen with an intentness which suggested that he hoped to read the answer for their problem somewhere within the maze of its drooping branches.

"Togi—" Charis broke the silence "—is she like Taggi? Could you call her?" What aid the wolverine might be Charis did not know, but to try and reach her was action of some sort, and just now she found inaction more frustrating than she could bear.

Exasperation sharpened Lantee's reply. "What do you think I'm trying to do? But since she has had cubs she is less receptive to orders. We have let her go her own way while they are small. Whether she will ever obey spoken commands again, I am not sure."

He closed his eyes, a frown line sharp between his well-marked brows. Charis propped her chin on her hand. As far as she could determine, the base continued to drowse in the sun. Was it really deserted? Through Wyvern Power sending its inhabitants into that strange darkness? Or left so by a Jack raid?

Unlike the rugged setting Jagan had chosen for his post, this more open country was lighter, gave no feeling of somberness darkening into possible menace. Or was she becoming so accustomed to the general Warlockian scenery that it no longer looked the same to her as it had when Jagan had brought her out of the spacer? How long ago? weeks? months? Charis had never been able to reckon how much time she had spent with the Wyverns.

Yes, here Warlock was fair under the amber sky, the golden sun. The amethystine hues of the foliage were sheer splendor. Purple and gold—the ancient colors of royalty in the days when Terra had hailed kings and queens, emperors and empresses. And now Terran blood had spread from star to star, mutated, adapted, even allegiances had changed from world to world as the tides of migration had continued generation after generation. Ander Nordholm had been born on Scandia, but she herself had never seen that planet. Her mother had been from Bran, and she herself could claim Minos for her native soil. Three widely separated and different worlds. And she could not remember Minos at all. Lantee—where had Shann Lantee been born?

Charis turned her head to study him, trying to select some race or planet to fit his name and his general physical appearance. But to her eyes he was not distinctive enough a type to recognize. Survey drew from almost every settled planet of the Confederation. He could even be a native Terran. That he was Survey meant that he had certain basic traits of character, certain very useful skills. And that he was also wearing the gold key of an embassy above his cadet bar meant even more—that he had extra-special attributes into the bargain.

"It's no use." He raised his hand to shade his now open eyes. "If she is still down there, I can't touch her —not mentally anyway."

"What did you think she might do to help us now?" Charis asked, curious.

"Maybe nothing." But that seemed an evasive answer to the girl.

"Are you a Beast Master?" she asked.

"No, Survey doesn't use animals that way—as fighters or sabotage teams. Taggi and Togi are both fighters when they have to be, but they act more as scouts. In lots of ways their senses are more acute than ours; they can learn more in a shorter time about a new stretch of country than any human. But Taggi and Togi were sent here originally as an experiment. We learned after the Throg attack just how much they could help—"

"Listen!" Charis's hand clamped onto his shoulder. She straightened out, flat to the ground, her head to one side. No, she had not been mistaken. The sound *was* growing louder.

"Atmosphere flyer!" Lantee's identification confirmed her own guess. "Back!" He rolled farther under the drooping branches of the bush and tugged at Charis as she wormed in after him.

The flyer was approaching from the north, not coming in over their present perch. As the plane set down on the landing strip, Charis saw that it was larger than the copter already there—probably a six-passenger ship motored for transcontinental service, not for the shorter flights of the copters.

"That's none of ours!" Lantee whispered.

It came to a halt and two men dropped from it to stride purposefully toward the domes. They went so confidently that the watchers knew they must expect welcome or at least believe that no difficulty awaited them. They were too far from the spy post for their features to be distinguished, but while they wore uniforms of a similar cut to those at the post, Charis had never seen these before. The black and silver of Patrol, the green-brown of Survey, the gray and red of the medical service, the blue of Administration, the plain green of the rangers, the maroon of Education—she could identify those at a glance. But these were a light yellow.

"Who?" she wondered. When she heard a small grunt from Lantee, she added, "Do you know?"

"Something—somewhere—" Then he shook his head. "I've seen something like that color, but I can't remember now."

"Would Jacks wear uniforms? The one I saw with the blaster—he was dressed just like any other Free Trader."

"No." Lantee's frown grew deeper. "It means something—if I could only remember!"

"No government service? Perhaps some planetary organization operating off-world," Charis suggested.

"I don't know how that could be. Look!"

A third man had come out of one of the domes. Like the two from the flyer he wore yellow, but sunlight struck glinting sparks from his collar and belt; that could only mark insignia of some type. A uniformed invasion of a government base— A wild idea suddenly struck Charis.

"Shann—could—could a war have broken out?"

For a moment he did not answer her and, when he did, it was almost as if he were trying to deny that idea to himself as much as to her.

"The only war we've waged in centuries has been against the Throgs—and those aren't Throgs down there! I was here just five days ago, and the messages we were receiving from off-world were all only routine. We had no warning of any trouble."

"*Five* days ago?" she challenged him. "How can we be sure of how much time passed while the Wyverns controlled us? It may have been weeks or longer since you were here."

"I know—I know. But I don't think war is the answer. I just don't believe it. But a Company action— If they thought they could get away with a grab— If the gain was big enough—"

Charis considered that. Yes, the Companies—they were regulated, curbed, investigated, as well as the Confederation and the Patrol could manage. But they had their own police, their extra-legal methods when they dared flaunt control. Only what would bring any one of the Companies to send a private army to Warlock? What treasure could be scooped up here before a routine Patrol visit would reveal such lawless activity?

"What could they find here to make it worth their while?" she asked. "Rare metals? What?"

"One thing—" Lantee continued to watch the men below. The two from the flyer were discussing something with the man from the dome. One of them broke away and headed back for the aircraft. "One thing might just be worth it if they could seize it."

"What?" Charis's guesses roved wildly. Surely Jagan would have known and mentioned any outstanding native product during his instruction on trading.

"The Power itself! Think what that secret would mean to men who could use it on other worlds!"

He was right. The Power was a treasure great enough to tempt even one of the Companies into piracy of a kind. If they mastered its use they could defy even the Patrol. And Lantee's idea fitted very neatly into place, especially now that she remembered Jagan's mention of the same quest.

"The nullifier." She thought aloud. "That's their answer to the use of the Power against *them*. But how did they develop something of the sort without knowing more about the Power? Maybe they believe they can use it to control the Wyverns and make them yield their secrets."

"The nullifier, whatever it is, can be an adaptation of

133

something already well known. As to the rest—yes—they could believe they have the witches finished."

"But the Jacks? Why?"

Lantee scowled. "Not the first time a Company has shoved some of its hard-fisted boys into plain clothes and tried a Jack cover-screen for a quick steal. If they're caught, then they're just Jacks and nothing else. If they succeed, the Company comes in behind their screen and they all fade out as soon as the grab is over. If they believe now that they've either wiped out all opposition or have it under wraps, then they're in the open with another force to consolidate their position and protect any experts and techs they send in for a real study of the Power. It all fits. Don't you see how it fits?"

"But—if this is a Company at work—" Charis's voice trailed off as the full force of what might be arrayed against them struck home.

"You're beginning to see? Jacks on their own are one thing; a Company pulling a grab is something else." Lantee's tone was bleak. "They will have resources to draw on to back their every move. Right now I wouldn't wager star against comet that they're not in complete control here."

"Maybe," Charis chose to use his gambling symbols, "they may believe that they have every comet on the board blocked, but there are a few wild stars left."

There was a faint suggestion of a smile about his lips.

"*Two* wild stars, perhaps?"

"Four. Do not underestimate Tsstu and Taggi." And she meant that, strange as it sounded.

"Four—you, me, a wolverine, and a curl-cat—against the might of a Company. You fancy high odds, don't you, Gentle Fem?"

"I fancy any odds we can get while the game is still

in play. The counters have not been swept from the board yet."

"No, nor the game called. And we might just run those odds to a more even balance. I do not think that our friends below have yet met the witches of Warlock. Even we do not know their full resources."

"I hope they have some good ones left," was her comment.

Only a short time ago the Wyverns had come out in the open as enemies. Now Charis wished with all her heart for their success. In the lines of battle, if what she and Lantee had come to believe was true, they would be on the side of the witches.

"What can we do?" She was again afire for action.

"We wait and still we wait. When it is dark, I want to see a little more of what is going on down there. Make sure, if we can, just what we are up against."

He was entirely right, but waiting now was so very hard.

XIII

THEY LAY side by side again, watching the base. The flyer had taken off, leaving behind one of its passengers; with the officer, he had returned to the domes. Again the site was seemingly deserted.

"That is a Patrol scout ship down there," Charis said. "Would any Company dare move outwardly against the patrol?"

"With a good cover story they could risk it," Lantee replied. "A scout isn't on a tight report schedule, remember. They could say that they found this base deserted and blame any trouble on the Wyverns if it became necessary to provide an explanation. What I'd like to know is—if this *is* a Company grab—how they came to learn of the Power. Jagan ever say anything about it?"

"Yes, he mentioned it once. But he spoke mostly about things such as this cloth." Charis plucked at the stuff of her tunic which was standing the hard usage better than Lantee's uniform. "He was gambling to make a high stake, but I thought trade material was mostly fishing on his part."

"He got in here over Thorvald's protest," Lantee commented. "We couldn't see how he rated a permit in the first place, he was so close to the fringe."

"Could he have been used as a Company cover? Maybe without his even knowing it?"

Lantee nodded. "Could well be. Send him in as an opening wedge and have his reports to add to their general knowledge since our files are closed—if any files are ever closed when the grab is big enough!" he ended cynically. "Somebody passed over a bag of credits in this deal. I'd swear blood-oath on that."

"Just what *can* you do down there?" Charis asked.

"If the com isn't out and if I can reach it, just one signal set on repeat will bring in such help as'll make these blaster merchants think someone's put a couple of earth-wasps under their tunic collars!"

"Several ifs in that."

Lantee smiled his humorless, lip-stretching smile. "Life is full of ifs, Gentle Fem. I've carried a pack of them for years."

"Where are you from, Shann?"

"Tyr." The answer was short, bitten off as if meant to be final.

"Tyr," Charis repeated. The name meant nothing to her, but who could ever catalogue the thousands of worlds where Terran blood had rooted, flowered, branched, and broken free to roam inward.

"Mining world. Right—right about there!" He had lifted his head and now he pointed northward into the sky which was displaying the more brilliant shades of sunset.

"I was born on Minos. But that doesn't mean much since my father was an Education officer. I've lived on—five—six—Demeter was the seventh world."

"Education officer?" Lantee echoed. "Then how did you get with Jagan? You beamed in a tape asking for aid. What was that all about anyway?"

She cut the story of Demeter and the labor contract to its bare bones as she told it.

"I don't know whether Jagan could have held you to that contract here on Warlock. On some worlds it'd be legal, but anyway you could have fought him with Thorvald's backing," he observed when she was done.

"Doesn't matter much now. You know—I didn't like Warlock at first. It—it was almost frightening. But now, even with all this, I want to stay here." Charis was surprised at her own words. She had said them impulsively but she knew they were true.

"By ordinary standards, this will never be a settlement world under the code."

"I know—intelligent native life over the fifth degree —so we stay out. How many Wyverns are there anyway?"

He shrugged. "Who knows? They must have more than one settlement among the off-shore islands, but we do not go except to their prime base and then only on permission. You perhaps know more about them than we do."

"This dreaming," Charis mused. "Who can be sure of anything with them? But can the Power really be used by males? They are so certain that it can't. And if they're right about that, what can the Company do?"

"Follow Jagan's lead and bring in women," he retorted. "But we're not sure that they are right. Maybe *their* males can't 'dream true,' as they express it, but I dreamed, and Thorvald did, when they put us through their test at first contact. Whether I could use a disk or pattern as you have I don't know. Their whole setup is so one-sided that contact with another way of life could push it entirely off base. Maybe if they were willing to try—"

"Listen!" Charis caught at his sleeve. Speculation about the future was interesting, but action was needed now. "What if you can use a pattern? You know the whole base; you could get down there and out again if you had to. It would be the perfect way to scout!"

Lantee stared at her. "If it did work—!" She watched him catch some of her enthusiasm. "If it just *would* work!"

He studied the base. The shadows cast by the domes were far more pronounced, though the sky was still bright over their heads. "I could try for my own quarters. But how would I get out again? There's no disk—"

"We'll have to make one or its equivalent. Let's see." Charis wriggled about under their brush cover. The initial pattern to get in by—she could draw that on the ground as she had before. But the other one—to bring Lantee out again—he'd have to carry that with him. How?

"Could you use this?" The Survey man pulled free a wide, dark leaf. Its purple surface was smooth save for a center rib and it was as big as her two hands.

"Try this to mark with." He had out his case of small tools and handed her a sharply pointed rod.

Carefully Charis traced the design which had unlocked so many strange places since she had first used it. Luckily the marks showed up well. When she had done, she handed the leaf to Lantee.

"It works so. First, you picture in your mind as clearly as you can the place you want to go. Then you concentrate on following this design with your eyes, from right to left—"

He glanced from the leaf to the base. "They can't be everywhere," he muttered.

Charis bit back a warning. Lantee knew the terrain better than she. Perhaps he, too, was chafing at inactivity. And, if the leaf pattern worked, he could be in and out of any danger before those who discovered him could move. It would be, or should be, sufficiently disconcerting to have a man materialize out of thin air before one, to give the materializer some seconds of advantage in any surprise confrontation.

Lantee's expression changed. He had made up his mind. "Now!"

Charis could not bring herself to agree in this final moment. As he had said earlier, there were so many ifs. But neither had she the right to persuade him not to make the try.

He slid down the slope behind them, putting the hill between him and the base before getting to his feet, the leaf in his hands. His jaw set, his whole face became a mask of concentration. Nothing happened. When he looked up at her, his expression was bleak and pinched.

"The witches are right. It won't work for me!"

139

"Perhaps—" Charis had another thought.

"They must be right! It didn't work."

"Maybe for another reason. That's *my* pattern, the one they gave me in the beginning."

"You mean the patterns are individual—separate codes?"

"It's reasonable to believe that. You know how they wear those decorative skin patterns, made up partially of their ancestors' private designs, in order to increase their own Power. But each of them has her disk with her own design on it. It could be that only that works really."

"Then I do it the hard way," he replied. "Go in after dark."

"Or I could go, if you'd give me a reference point as you did when we came here."

"No!" There was no arguing against that; she read an adamant refusal in his whole stance.

"Together—as we came here?"

He balanced the leaf in his hand. Charis knew that he longed to be as decisive with another "no," but there were advantages in her second suggestion which he had to recognize. She pushed that indecision quickly; not that she had any desire to penetrate into the enemy's camp, but neither did she want to remain here alone and perhaps witness Lantee's capture. To her mind, with the Power the two of them would have a better chance working together than the Survey man had as a lone scout.

"We can get in—and out—in a hurry. You've already agreed that's true."

"I don't like it."

She laughed. "What *can* one like about this? It is something we have agreed must be done. Or shall we just

140

take to the countryside and wait out whatever they are planning to do?" Such prodding was not fair of her, but her impatience was rising to a point where it threatened her control.

"All right!" He was angry. "The room is like this." Down on one knee, he sketched out a plan, explaining curtly. Then, before she could move, those same brown fingers were against her forehead, giving her once more that fuzzy picture. Charis jerked away from that contact.

"I told you—not that! Not again!" The girl had no desire to recall any of the earlier dizzy, frightening time when they joined minds after a fashion, when the strange thoughts strove to storm her own mental passages.

Lantee flushed and drew his hand back. Her uneasiness and faint disgust were at once overlaid by a feeling of guilt. After all, he was doing the best he could to insure the success of their action.

"I have the picture now as clearly as I had this place, and we came here safely," she said hurriedly. "Let's go!" For a moment his hand resisted her grasp as she caught it, then his hold tightened on hers.

First the room—then the pattern. It was becoming a familiar exercise, one she had full confidence in. But now—*nothing happened.*

It was as if she had thrown herself against some immovable and impenetrable wall! The barrier the Wyverns had reared to control her movements earlier? It was not that. She would have known it for what it was. This was different—a new sensation altogether.

She opened her eyes. "Did you feel it?" Lantee might not be able to work the transference on his own; but, linked, they had done it successfully once, so perhaps some part of the present failure had reached him.

"Yes. You know what it means? They do have a nullifier to protect them!"

"And it works!" Charis shivered, her hand creasing the leaf into a pulp.

"We were already sure that it did," he reminded her. "Now—I shall go by myself."

She did not want to admit that he was right, but she had to. Lantee knew every inch of the base; she was a stranger there. The invaders might have other safeguards besides the nullifier.

"You don't even have a stunner . . ."

"If I can get in down there, that little matter can be corrected. More than a stunner is needed now. This you *can* do—work your way around to the landing strip. If I succeed, we'll make use of the copter. You can fly one?"

"Of course! But where will we go?"

"To the Wyverns. They'll have to be made to understand what they are up against here. I ought to find evidence of one kind or another as to whether this is a Company grab. The witches may be able to blanket you out of their own mode of travel, but I'll swear they have no way of preventing the copter from reaching their prime base. Let us just get to them and they can pick the truth out of our minds whether they want to or not."

It sounded simple and as if it might work, Charis had to admit. But there was that tall hedge of ifs in between.

"All right. When do we move?"

Lantee crawled up to their former vantage point and she trailed him. After he surveyed the landscape he spoke, but he did not answer her question.

"You circle around in that direction, giving me a hundred-count start. We haven't spotted any guards about the strip, but that doesn't mean that they haven't plugged it with sniffers, and those might even be paired with anti-persona bombs into the bargain."

Was he deliberately trying to make her regret any part in this?

"We could certainly use the wolverines now. No sniffer could baffle them," he continued.

"We could use a detachment of the Patrol, too," Charis retorted tartly.

Lantee did not rise to that. "I'll come in from that direction." He pointed south. "Let's hope our wild stars have the value we hope they do on this board. Luck!"

Before she could more than blink he had gone, vanished into the brush as if one of the disks had whirled him into Otherwhere. Charis strove to fight down her excitement and began a slow count. For some seconds she heard a subdued rustling which she was sure marked his retreat—then nothing.

No movement about the domes. Lantee was right; they *could* have used the wolverines and Tsstu to advantage now. Animal senses, so much keener than human, could have scouted for them both. She thought of an anti-persona bomb twinned to a sniffer detector, and her own part in the action had less and less appeal. The copter was far too tempting a bait; those below *must* have some watch on it! Unless they believed that they had effectively disposed of all resistance.

"—ninety-five—ninety-six—" Charis counted, hoping she was not speeding up. It was always far easier to be on the move than to lie and wait.

"—ninety-nine—one-hundred!" She crept down slope to the east on the first lap of her own journey. The light held enough so that she kept to cover, pausing within each shadowed shelter to study the next few feet or

143

yards of advance. And, to keep in concealment, she pulled her circle arc into a segment of oval. When she knew that she must head in again to meet the landing strip, Charis's mouth was dry in contrast to her damp palms, while her heart thudded in a heavy beat.

She found a tree limb, old and brittle—dry but long enough for her purpose. A sniffer activated to catch a prowler would be set about so high—knee-high for a walking man—or less. Would they expect someone to crawl in? All right, then, to be on the safe side—calf-high Charis set about stripping small branches for handfuls of leaves. Several tough ground-vines gave her cords to lash the mass of vegetation to the stick.

As a device for triggering a trap, it was very crude, but it lessened the odds against her somewhat. Now her wriggling advance was even slower as she worked the bundle before her, testing each foot of the way.

The pole was hard to hold in her sweating hands, her shoulders ached with the effort necessary to keep it at what she believed to be the right height. And her goal could have been half the continent away since she appeared to draw no closer to it in spite of her continued struggles.

But so far—no sniffer. And there had to be an end sometime. Charis paused for a breather. No sound came from the domes, no indication there were any guards, either human or machine. Were the invaders under the impression they had nothing to fear, no reason to post sentries?

Must not let growing confidence make her careless, Charis told herself. She did not have one hand on the copter door yet. And—why!—that might be it! The machine itself could be rigged as a trap. And if that were so, could she discover and disarm it?

One thing at a time—just one thing at a time . . .

She had raised her bundle probe, was on the creep again when the twilight breeze brought her a faint scent. Wolverine! When aroused in fear or anger, Charis knew, the animals emitted a rank odor. Was this a mark of the passing of Togi and her cubs?

Could Charis contact the female wolverine who had no knowledge of her as friendly? Lantee had said that afternoon that Togi was less amenable to human contact or control since she had become a mother; the wolverines were noted hunters, accustomed to living off the land. Was Togi now hunting?

Charis sniffed, hoping for some clue as to direction. But the scent was faint, perhaps only a lingering reminder of some earlier passage of an angry wolverine clinging to grass or bush. And there stood the beacon of the Patrol scout not too far to her left. She was close to the fringe of the landing strip. Charis thrust her bundle detector before her and crept on.

A screech—a snarling—a thrashing in the brush to her left. A second cry cut into a horrible bubbling noise.

Charis bit her tongue, painfully muffling a cry of her own. Wide-eyed she watched that wildly waving bush. Another cry—this time not unlike a thin, pulsating whistle. Then suddenly there were figures out in the open, running toward the commotion. As they neared, Charis could see them better.

Not the off-worlders she and Lantee had watched from the hill. Wyverns? No.

For the second time, Charis choked back a cry. For these running figures carried spears, the same type of spear she and Lantee had found at the post. And they were taller than the Wyverns Charis knew, their spiky head and shoulder growths smaller so that they resembled ragged and ugly spines rather than small wings: the Wyvern males Charis had never seen in all her days among the witches!

They cried out shrilly in a way which rasped Charis's nerves and hurt her ears. Two of them hurled spears into the now quiet bush.

A shout from behind, from the domes; this surely had issued from a human throat. No words Charis could distinguish but it bought confusion to the Wyverns. The two at the rear stopped, looked over their shoulders; then, at a second shout, they turned and ran swiftly in the direction of that call. The foremost attackers had reached the bushes, spears thrust ahead. One of them cried out. Again no words, but Charis judged the tone to be one of disappointment and rage.

They milled around out of her sight and then came back into the open, two of them carrying a limp body between them. One of their own kind killed by some means. Togi's doing?

But Charis had little time to wonder about that for there was more shoutihg from the domes, and all but the two Wyverns carrying the body began to run in that direction.

Lantee—had they found Lantee?

XIV

THE WYVERN males had left the landing strip. Charis could follow their path through the brush to the open and the waiting copter. Lantee's plan of heading out to

146

sea in the copter, aiming at the witch Citadel, was practical. Lantee?

Charis rubbed her hands together and tried to think clearly. Something had happened back there at the domes; it was only logical to associate the clamor with Lantee's attempt to scout the enemy. He could now be a prisoner—or worse.

But if she took the copter now when the attention of any sentries was fixed elsewhere, she had her best chance of escape, though she might well be deserting a man who had aroused the invaders but managed to evade them. To go—to get to the Citadel and warn the witches of the possible danger, leaving Lantee, his fate unknown? Or to stay in hopes of his coming?

There was no real choice; there never had been, Charis knew that deep within her. But now, at the final test, she felt as bruised and beaten as if those spear carriers had taken her in an unequal struggle. Somehow she got to her feet and ran for the copter.

As she wrenched open the cockpit door, Charis paused for any trap to explode in her face. Then she scrambled in behind the controls. So far, all right. Now—where?

The Citadel was to the west, that was her only clue. Only, the sea was wide and she had never made the journey by air, as Lantee had. Maybe her guide could be a negative one, and she tracked her goal by the barrier against the Power or rather her use of it. Such a thin chance—but still a chance.

Charis set the control on full, braced herself for the force of a lift-leap, and pushed the proper button. She was slammed back in the cushioned pilot's chair. Copters were not designed for such violent maneuvering. But a lift-leap would take her off the strip with speed enough to startle any guard she had not seen.

She gulped and fought the effects of the spurt upon her body, forcing her fingers to modify the climb. The domes were now small silvery circles just visible in the growing dark. She set a course northward, and put the flyer temporarily on auto-pilot while she tried to think out just how she could track that barrier with any accuracy.

How did you track nothingness? Just try to pierce here and there until you found the wall between you and your goal? Her vague direction was that island home of the Wyverns which stood northwest of the government base, southwest from Jagan's post, and she had not even a com sweep to give her a more definite position.

Below, just visible in the night, was the shore, an irregular division between land and sea. The pattern—she *must* have the pattern. Charis looked about her a little wildly. There was no leaf to scratch, no earth or rock to draw upon. That wall storage pocket at her left hand? Charis plunged fingers into it and spilled out what it contained.

A packet of Sustain tablets—swiftly she scooped that into her own belt pouch and another first-aid kit, bigger and better fitted than the small one Lantee had carried. Joyfully Charis scrabbled in it for the sterile pencil. It was not here, but there was a large tube of the same substance. Last of all, a flat sheet of plasta-board such as could be used for sketch maps, its surface slightly roughened as if it had been marked and erased many times.

This would serve if she could find something with which to mark. Again Charis pawed into the pocket, and her fingers, scraping the bottom of the holder, closed about a thin cylinder. She brought out a fire tube. No use—or was it?

Frantically she twisted its dial to the smallest ray,

and pressed the tip tight to the plasta-board. It was such a chance—the whole thing might go up in a burst of flame. But a map sheet should have been proofed against heat as well as moisture. Only this one had been used in the past, perhaps too often. She drew swiftly, fearful of any mistake. The brown heat-lines bit deeply into the surface and spread a little, but not enough to spoil the design.

Charis clicked off the heat unit and studied what she now held. Blurred, yes, but to her distinctive enough in its familiarity. She had a good substitute for the disk which she had lost.

Now—to put it to use. She closed her eyes. The room in the Citadel—concentrate!—the barrier! But in which direction? All she knew was that the barrier still existed. Her one idea of a direction-finder seemed a failure. No one gave up at a first try, though.

Room—design—barrier. Charis opened her eyes. Her head was turned slightly to the left. Was that a clue? Could she test it? She snapped the copter off auto-pilot and altered course inland away from the shore. When she had ceased to see the sea with only the dark mass of land now under her, she brought the flyer about and cruised back.

Room—design— Her head to the left again, but not so much. She had to take that as her lead, slender as it was. Altering the degree of course to that imagined point, she sent the copter on out to sea.

Design—try— She was looking straight ahead when she met what she could not penetrate. Oh, let this *be* right. *Let it be right.*

Charis had no idea how far offshore the Wyvern-held islands were. Any copter had a good ranging allowance, but her goal might still lie hours ahead. She clicked up

149

the speed to full and sat with her hands on the map sheet, waiting.

The stars were low on the horizon. No! Not stars— they were far too low. Lights! Lights at nearly sea level —the Citadel! On impulse Charis tried the Power and it was as if she had thrown her body at full force against an unyielding slab of tri-steel. She gasped at what was translated into physical pain upon that encounter.

But the copter had met with no barrier. It continued on, unerringly bound for the lights ahead.

Charis had no idea what she would do when she reached the Citadel. Only she had her warning, and with the Power the Wyverns would know that she spoke the truth. Even with the warning—what could the witches do in their turn, except avoid outright and quick disaster by delaying whatever attack they had already organized.

The lights picked out the windows in the massive block of the Citadel, some of them almost on a level with the copter. Charis resumed control and circled the buildings in search of a level site on which to land. She had rounded the highest of the blocks when she sighted ground lights marking an open space, almost as if they had prepared for her coming.

As the flyer touched the pavement, she saw a second copter at one side. So—the other Survey man, Thorvald, had not left. An ally for her? Or was he now a prisoner, tucked away in such a pocket of nonbeing as Lantee had been? Lantee— Charis tried to push out of her mind any thought of Lantee.

She held the plasta-board. In this well-like space between walls there were no breaks, no doors, and the windows were at least a story above her. The lights which had directed her landing burned in portable standards.

So the Wyverns *had* expected her. Yet no one waited here; she might be standing in a trap.

Charis nodded. This was all a part of what the shadow-patterned Wyvern had promised. She must do it all by her own efforts; the answer had to be *hers*.

The shadow Wyvern had said it, so to her it must be proven. Charis held the plasta-board in her two hands where she could see its design in the flickering half-light of the lamps. Spike-wing crest, pallid skin with only the faint tracings of faded designs—Charis pulled the Wyvern out of memory and built with care the picture to center upon, until she was sure no detail she could recall was missing. Then—

"So you *can* dream to a purpose after all." No amazement, only recognition as a greeting.

The room was dusky. Although two lamps stood on either side of a table, their radiance made only a small pool, and Charis sensed larger space stretching far beyond where she stood. That other—the Wyvern—sat in a chair with a high back, its white substance glowing with runnels of color, which in themselves appeared to crawl with life.

She leaned back at her ease, the alien witch, her hands resting on the arms of her chair as she surveyed Charis appraisingly. Now the off-worlder found words to answer.

"I have dreamed to this much purpose, Wise One, that I stand here now."

"Agreed. And to what future purpose do you stand here, Dreamer?"

"That a warning may be delivered."

The vertical pupils in those large yellow eyes narrowed, the snouted head raised a fraction of an inch, and the sense of affront reached Charis clearly.

"You have that which will arm you against us, Dreamer? Then you *have* made a gain since last we were thus, face to face. What great new power have you discovered to be able to say 'I warn you' to us?"

"You mistake my words, Wise One. I do not warn you against myself, but against others."

"And again you take upon yourself more than you have the right to do, Dreamer. Have you then read your answer from Those Gone Before?"

Charis shook her head. "Not so. But still you mistake me, Reader of Patterns. In what is to come, we dream one dream, not dream against dream."

Those eyes searched into her, seemed to pick at her mind.

"It is true that you have done more than we believed you could, Dreamer. Yet you are not one with us in any power save that which we have granted you. Why do you presume to say that we are now to dream the same dream?"

"Because if we do not, then may all dreams be broken."

"And that you truly believe." Not a question but a statement. However, Charis made a quick answer.

"That I truly believe."

"Then you have learned more than how to break a restraint dream since last we have stood together. What have you learned?"

"That those from off-world are more powerful than we thought, that they have with them that which renders all dreams as nothing and protects them, that *their* desire here may be to gather to them the Power that they may use it for their own purposes in other places."

Again that faint pick, pick to uncover the truth behind her words. Then, "But of these facts you are not wholly sure."

"Not wholly," Charis agreed. "Every pattern is made of lines. So, when you have long known a design and see only a portion of it, you can still envision the whole."

"And this is a pattern you have known before?"

"It is one I have heard of, one Lantee has heard of."

Had she made a mistake in mentioning the Survey man's name? That chill which reached from mind to mind suggested that she had.

"What has any man-thing to do with this?" A hissing question hot with rising ire.

Charis's anger woke in turn. "This much, Wise One. He may be dead now, striving to carry war to the enemy —*your* enemy!"

"How can that be when he is—" The thought chain between them broke in mid-sentence. Lids dropped above the yellow eyes. The feeling of withdrawal was so sharp that Charis almost expected the Wyvern to vanish from her chair. Yet her body was still there although her mind was elsewhere.

The minutes were endless, then Charis knew the Wyvern had returned. Fingers had clenched about the chair arms, the yellow eyes were open, fixed upon the girl, though there was no touch of mind.

Charis took a chance. "You did not find him, Wise One, where you had sent him?"

No answer, but Charis was sure the Wyvern understood.

"He is not there," the girl continued, "nor has he been for some time. As I told you in truth, he has been about *your* business elsewhere. And perhaps to his hurt."

"He did not free himself." The frantic grip of the Wyvern's hands relaxed. Charis thought that the witch was annoyed because she had betrayed her agitation so much. "He could not. He is a man-thing—"

153

"But also a dreamer after his own fashion," Charis struck in. "And though you strove to remove him from this struggle, yet he returned—not to war against you but against those who threaten all dreaming."

"What dream have you that you can do this thing?"

"Not my dream alone," Charis retorted. "But his dream also, and other dreams together, as a key to unlock this prison."

"I must believe that this is so. Yet such an act is beyond all reason."

"All reason known to you and your sharers of dreams. Look, you." Charis moved to the table, stretched out hand and arm into the full path of the light. "Am I like unto you in the sight of all? Do I wear any dream patterns set upon my skin? Yet I dream. However, need my dreams be any more like unto yours than my body covering resembles that you wear? Perhaps even the Power when I bend it to my will is not the same."

"Words—"

"Words with proving action behind them. You sent me hence and bade me dream myself out of your net if I could, and so I did. Then with Shann Lantee I dreamed a way free from a deeper prison. Did you believe I could do these things?"

"Believe? No," the Wyvern replied. "But there is always a chance of difference, a variable within the Power. And the Talking Rods had an answer for you when we called upon Those Who Once Were. Very well, these are truths accepted. Now say again what you believe to be a truth that had no full proving."

Charis retold her discoveries at the base, Lantee's deductions.

"A machine which nullifies the Power." The Wyvern led her back to that. "Such you believe *can* exist?"

"Yes. Also—what if such a thing be brought to use against you even in this very stronghold? With your dreams broken, how may you fight against slaying weapons in the hands of those who come?"

"We knew—" the Wyvern was musing "—that we could not send dreams to trouble these strangers. Or bring back—" she spoke in anger "—to their proper places those who have broken the law. But that all this is being done so that they may take the Power from us—that we had not thought upon."

Charis knew a small spark of relief. That last admission had changed her own status. It was as if she were now admitted in a small way into the Wyvern ranks.

"However, they must be ignorant to believe that man-things can use the Power."

"Lantee does," Charis reminded her. "And what of the other you have known as a friend here—Thorvald?"

Hesitation, then an unwilling answer. "He, too, in a small way. An ability, you believe, that these others may share because they are not blood, bone, and skin with us?"

"Is that so hard to understand?"

"And what have you to suggest, Dreamer? You speak of battles and warfare. Our only weapons have been our dreams, and now you say they will avail nothing. So—what is your answer?" Hostility again.

And Charis had little with which to meet that. "What these invaders do here is against the law of our kind as much as it is a threat against your people. There are those who will speedily come to our aid."

"From where? Winging down from other stars? And how will you call them? How long will it take them to arrive?"

"I do not know. But you have the man Thorvald, and he would have answers to these questions."

"It would seem, Dreamer, that you believe I, Gidaya, can give all orders here, do as I wish. But that is not so. We sit in council. And there are those among us who would not listen to any truth if you spoke it. We have been divided upon this matter from the first, and to talk against attacking now will require much persuasion. Should you stand openly with me, that persuasion would fail."

"I understand. But also, as you have said to me, Wise One, there is such a thing as a threat by time. Let me speak to Thorvald if you have him here, and learn from him what may be done to gain help from off-world." Had she gone too far with that plea?

Gidaya did not answer at once. "Thorvald is in safe keeping—" she paused and then added "—though I wonder now about the safety of any keeping. Very well, you may go to him. It may be that I shall say to those who will object that you are joining him in custody."

"If you wish." Charis suspected that Gidaya would offer that as a sop to the anti-off-world party. But she greatly doubted that the Wyvern believed any longer Charis herself could be controlled by the Power.

"Go!"

At least Thorvald had not been consigned to that place of nothingness which had been Lantee's prison. Charis stood in a very ordinary sleeping room of the Citadel, its only difference from the one she had called her own being that it had no window. On the pile of sleep-mats lay a man, breathing heavily. His head turned and he muttered, but she could not make out his words.

"Thorvald! Ragnar Thorvald!"

The bronze-yellow head did not lift from the mats nor his eyes open. Charis crossed to kneel beside him.

"Thorvald!"

He was muttering again. And his hand balled into a fist and shot out to thud home painfully on her forearm. Dreaming! Naturally? Or in some fantasy induced by the Wyverns? But she must wake him now.

"Thorvald!" Charis called louder and took hold of his shoulder, shaking him vigorously.

He struck out again, sending her rolling back against the wall, then sat up, his eyes open at last, looking about wildly. But as he sighted her he tensed.

"You're real—I think!" His emphatic assertion slid into a less confident conclusion.

"I'm Charis Nordholm." She crouched against the wall, rubbing her arm. "And I'm real all right. This is no dream."

No, no dream but the worst of trouble. And did Thorvald have any of the answers after all? She only hoped that he did.

XV

HE WAS very tall, this officer of Survey, towering over Charis where she sat cross-legged on his mat bed as he strode impatiently back and forth across the chamber, now and then shooting a question at her or making her retell some part of the story again.

"It does look very much like a Company grab." He gave judgment at last. "Which means they must be very sure of themselves, that they think they have all angles covered." Now he might be talking to himself rather than to her. "A deal—somehow they've made a deal!"

Charis guessed at the meaning of that. "You think they've arranged for closed eyes somewhere?"

Thorvald glanced at her sharply, almost in dislike, Charis decided. But he nodded curtly. "Not in our service!" he rapped out.

"But they wouldn't be able to square the Patrol, would they? Not if you were able to get a message through."

He smiled grimly. "Hardly. But the only off-world com is at the base, and from your account they hold that now."

"There's the Patrol ship finned down on the field. That should have its own com," she pointed out.

Thorvald rubbed one hand along the angle of his jaw, his eyes now fixed unseeingly on the blank wall of the chamber.

"Yes, that Patrol ship—"

"They didn't have any guard on the copter."

"They weren't expecting trouble then. They probably thought they had all the base staff accounted for. That wouldn't be true now."

She could see the reason in that argument. Yes, when they had taken Lantee, as she was now sure they had, and she had flown the copter out, they had been put on the alert. If the Patrol ship had not been guarded before, Charis did not doubt now that it was under strict surveillance.

"What can we do?"

"We'll have to count on it that they do have Lantee."

Or, Charis made herself add silently to Thorvald's statement, he is dead.

"And they know that he had at least one other with

him, since the copter was taken. They may scan him, and he's not been brain-locked."

Charis found her hands shaking. There was a cold sickness in her middle, seeping into the rest of her body. Thorvald was only being objective, but she found she could not be the same on this point, not when the man he was discussing was more than a name—a living person who, in a way Charis could hardly describe, had been closer to her than any other being she had known. She was unaware that the Survey officer had paused until he dropped down beside her, his hands covering both of hers.

"We must face the truth," he said quietly.

Charis nodded, her spine stiffened, and her head came up. "I know. But I went off—off and left him—"

"Which was the only thing you could have done. He knew that. Also, there is this. Those male Wyverns—they were attacked by something in the bush—you think it was Togi?"

"I smelled wolverine just before. And one of the Wyverns was killed, or badly injured."

"Which may lead them to believe that there were more than two of you out there. And that could force caution on them. The animals work with trainers—that is universally known. And it's also general knowledge that they are fanatically loyal to their trainers. Lantee has been in charge of the wolverines for two planet years. Those at the base may keep him on ice in order to have control over the animals."

Did he really believe that? Charis wondered. Or was it a very thin attempt to placate her feelings of guilt?

"This nullifier," Thorvald was on his feet again, back to that restless pacing. "As long as they have that they might as well be in a land fortress! And how long will they wait before moving out with it? If they had a trace-beam on that copter, they know—"

"Just where to attack!" Charis finished for him, realizing for the first time what might be the folly of her own move.

"You had no choice." Thorvald caught her up on that quickly. "A warning was important. And with the Wyvern barrier up you had no other way of reaching them."

"No, but I have a way of getting back there." Charis had been thinking. It was a crazy, wild plan, but it might work. She had his full attention.

Sheeha! Charis had gone back to her first night on Warlock, to the trader woman who had been shocked into mental unbalance by contact with the witches.

"These invaders know that Jagan brought me here," Charis began. "Also that I wandered out of the post while under Wyvern control; they can check all that. They might even have the tape recording I made to your base when I appealed for help. But it may be that they do not know that *I* took the copter. Or, if they do—well, how much do they know of the Power? They know the Wyverns used it to dominate and control their males. So, perhaps they will think I was under Wyvern control while taking the copter.

"Now, suppose I let them think I have escaped and that I have headed back to the base because I think there is safety there. I can act as Sheeha did."

"And if they put you under a scanner?" Thorvald demanded harshly, "or if they have already learned from Lantee what you can do with the Power?"

"If they have, they won't want me under a scanner, not right away. They'll want demonstrations," Charis countered. "They can't know too much about it, can they?

What have you reported? Those reports must have brought them here."

"Reports? What have we had to say in those except generalities? We had our instructions to go slow with the witches. After they helped us wipe out a Throg base here—it was entirely their efforts that broke that—they were in no hurry to fraternize. The willingness to communicate had to come from their side, contact was on a delicate basis. I don't understand about this nullifier. No off-world Company could have learned enough from our reports to build it because we didn't know enough ourselves. Unless this machine is a modification of something they already had and they brought it with them, simply as an experiment which did pay off—too well!"

"Then," said Charis, bringing him back to her own suggestion, "they could not know about the Power and how it works?"

"I don't see how they could. They may have subverted some of the male Wyverns. But those have never been able to dream or use the Power. Company scouts could have some idea of what it does, but they'd only be guessing at how it works."

"So as an off-worlder who has had some experience with it, I could make statements they would have no way of testing?"

"Unless they use a scanner," he reminded her.

"But when you're dealing with a mental problem, you don't destroy its roots," Charis countered. "I tell you, if I went to them as a fugitive who had escaped the Wyverns and was willing to co-operate, anyone with any intelligence would not put me under force. He would want me to give freely."

Thorvald studied her. "There's more than one kind of

force," he said slowly. "And if they suspected that you were playing a double game, they wouldn't hesitate to use all and every means to crack you for what they wanted. A Company on a grab is moving against time, and their agents here would be ruthless."

"All right. Then what's *your* answer? It seems that I have the best chance of getting into the base on my own terms. Do you or the witches have any at all? If you're taken trying to get in—the way Shann was—then you're expendable too."

"Yes."

"Well, I represent something they want—an off-worlder who has had experience with the use of the Power. There is a good chance to get close to the nullifier under those circumstances. And if I could put that out of action, then the witches could do the rest. As it is now, the Wyverns suspect us too, just because we are off-world."

"And how can you convince the Wyverns that you will work against our own species?"

"They read my mind under the Power. There's no hiding the truth from them. Short of leading in an armed force, which we don't have, you aren't going to take back your base. And someone has to make a move before the invaders do."

"You don't know how rough a grab force can be—" Thorvald began.

Charis stood up. "I have been hunted by men before. You can tell me very little about cruelty used as a weapon. But as long as I present a chance of profit to those in command, I shall be guarded. And I think that now I am your only key."

The girl closed her eyes for a second. This was fear, this sick chill. Yes, she knew what it meant to face hostility;

before, she had to run from it. Now she must walk defenseless straight into the worst her imagination could picture for her. But there *was* a chance. She had known that from the argument she had had with Gidaya. Perhaps the continued use of the Power did implant in one a confidence. Only, once at the base, she would not have the Power to pull on; the nullifier would see to that. She would have only her wits and luck to back her. Or—could she have more? The wolverines, Togi and her cubs, lurked about the base, apparently free of control and able to prey upon the alien guards. Charis had had no contact with Togi, but with Taggi, who had been so strangely one with her in that search for Lantee, and with Tsstu, it might be different. Where were the animals now?

"You have something more in mind?" A change in her expression must have brought that question from him.

"Tsstu and Taggi—" she began and then explained more fully.

"But I don't understand. You say that they weren't with you in the Cavern of the Veil or afterward."

"No, but they answered when we called. I don't think they were captive in any dream place. Perhaps they had to be free to go their own way for a space after that. It —it was a frightening experience." Charis had a flash thought of the corridor, the opening doors in which Lantee's thoughts had attacked her, and again she shivered. "They may have run from what they remembered."

"Then—will they return?"

"I think they will have to," Charis said simply. "We wove a bond then and still it holds us. Maybe we can never loose it. But if I could find them, they would be allies those at the base would not suspect."

"Suppose the nullifier dampened contact between you?" Thorvald persisted.

"If I reached them before I went in, they would know what they could do in aid."

"You seem to have all the answers!" He did not appear to relish that admission. "So you're to walk alone into a trap and spring it—just like that!"

"Maybe I can't. But I believe there's no other solution."

"Again you read the pattern right, Sharer of Dreams!"

They looked around, startled. Gidaya stood there and with her, Gysmay.

Thorvald opened his mouth, then closed it again. There was a set to his jaw that suggested that, while he knew silence was proper, he resented it.

"You are persuaded it must be thus?" Charis asked of the Wyverns.

Gysmay made a movement of the shoulders approximating a human shrug.

"I, who am a Holder of the Upper Disk, will go with the desires of my Sharers of Dreams in this matter. You believe, one who is not quite a stranger, that this is what must be done. And you are willing to take that doing into your own hands. So let it be. Though we cannot give you any aid, since the evil which has been brought to trouble our world holds about its heart a wall we cannot pierce."

"No, you cannot aid me once I am within that place. But there is that you can do for me before I enter—"

"Such being?" Gidaya asked.

"That Tsstu and Taggi be found and summoned from where they have gone."

"Tsstu at least has power of a sort, but whether that may be harnessed to your purpose—" the older Wyvern hesitated. "However, no power, no aid, is to be despised when one walks into a fork-tail's den without a disk between one's fingers. Yes, we shall search out the small one and also the other who serves these men. Perchance we can do more, using like tools—"

Gysmay nodded eagerly. "That is a good thought, Reader of the Rods! One can build on it. Perchance we can provide some action for these invaders to think upon so that their minds will be in two ways occupied and not fastened alone upon you and what you would do among them. We cannot walk through their rooms, but we shall see." She did not elaborate.

Turning to Charis, Thorvald cut in: "I'm going with you—in the copter."

"You can't!" Charis protested. "I won't take the flyer back. I must wander in as if I have been lost—"

"I didn't say land at the base. But I must be back near the base, near enough to be able to move in when we can." He said that defiantly, glaring at the Wyverns as if he would compel them to his will.

When we can, Charis thought, more likely—*if* we can.

"It is well," Gidaya answered, though there was a small movement from Gysmay as if she were protesting. "Take your machine and fly—to this place—"

Into Charis's mind came instantly a clear picture of a flat rock expanse squared off to make a natural landing strip.

"About a mile from the base!" Thorvald burst out; he must also have had that mind picture and recognized it. "We shall come in from the south—at night—without landing lights. I can set us down there without trouble."

"And Tsstu—Taggi?" demanded Charis of the Wyverns.

"They shall join you there for whatever purpose you think they may serve. Now you may go."

Charis was back in the landing well where the two

copters were waiting, but this time Thorvald was with her. As the girl started for the machine which had brought her to the Citadel, the Survey officer caught at her arm.

"Mine—not that one." He drew her with him toward the other copter. "If it's sighted after we land, they'll believe I returned and am hiding out. They won't connect it with you."

Charis agreed to the sense of that and watched him settle behind the controls as she took her place on the second seat. They lifted with a leap which signaled his impatience more than his words had done. Then, under the night sky, they drove on, the ocean below them.

"They may have a search beam on," he said as his fingers played a dot-dash over course buttons. "We'll take the long way around to make sure we have the best cover we can. North—then west—then up from the south—"

It *was* a long way around. Charis watched with eyes over which the lids were growing very heavy. The smooth sheen of the night-darkened sea underneath them spread on and on in spite of their speed. To be flying away from their goal instead of toward it was hard to be reconciled to now.

"Settle back," Thorvald's voice was low and even; he now had his own impatience under iron control. "Sleep if you can."

Sleep? How could anyone sleep with such a task before her. Sleep—that . . . was . . . impossible . . .

Dark—thick, negative dark. Negative? What did that mean? Dark, and then, deep in the heart of that blackness, a small fire struggling to beat back the dark A fire threatened, a fire she must reach and feed. Bring it back

166

to bright blaze again! But when Charis strove to speed to the fire, she could move only with agonizing slowness, so that the weight which dragged at her limbs was a pain in itself. And the fire flickered, reblazed, and then flickered. Charis knew that when it died wholly it might not be relit. But she needed more than herself to feed that fire, and she sent out a frantic, soundless call for aid. There was no answer.

"Wake up!"

Charis's body swayed in a rough grip, her head jerked back and forth on her shoulders. She looked up, blinking and half-dazed, into eyes which blazed with some of the intensity of the fire of the dark.

"You were dreaming!" It was an accusation. "They have a hold on you. They never meant—"

"No!" Enough understanding had returned to make her shake off thorvald's hands. "Not one of *their* dreams."

"But you *were* dreaming!"

"Yes." She huddled in the copter seat as the machine flew on under auto-pilot. "Shann—"

"What about him?" Thorvald caught her up quickly.

"He's still alive." Charis had brought that one small crumb of assurance out of the black with her. "But—"

"But what?"

"He's just holding on." That, too, had come to her although it was not so reassuring. What had strained Lantee to the depths she had witnessed? Physical hurt? A scanner attack? He was alive and he was still fighting. That she knew with certainty and now she said so.

"No real contact? He told you nothing?"

"Nothing. But I almost reached him. If I could try again—".

"No!" Thorvald shouted at her. "If he is under a scanner, you don't know how much they could pick up because of such a contact. You—you'll have to put him out of your mind."

Charis only looked at him.

"You'll have to," he repeated doggedly. "If they pick you up in any way, you haven't a chance of going in as you've planned. Can't you see? You are the only chance Lantee has now. But you'll have to reach him in person in order to help; not this way!"

Thorvald was right. Charis had enough sense left to acknowledge that rightness, though that did not make it any easier when she thought of the small fire flickering close to extinction in a deep and all-abiding darkness.

"Hurry!" She moistened her dry lips with her tongue. He was resetting their course. "Yes."

The copter spiraled away to the right, heading toward the shore they could not see and the task she had set herself.

XVI

THE STARS were no longer sharp points above as the copter set down under Thorvald's practiced control. An hour close to dawn—Dawn of what day? Time had either stretched slowly or fled swiftly since Charis had walked out onto the soil of Warlock. She could no longer be sure that it followed any ordered marking of minutes or hours. She stood now on the rock, shivering a little in the chill predawn wind.

"Meeerrrreee!" At the cry of welcome, Charis went

down on her knees, holding out her arms to the shadow which sped toward her. The warmth of that small body pressing tight to hers, the loving dabs of tongue-tip against her throat, her chin, brought a measure of comforting confidence. Tsstu was again in the circle of Charis's arms, avid for contact, excited in her welcome.

Then the rasp of harsher, coarser fur against the girl's legs signaled Taggi's arrival. A small grunting growl was his vocal hail as she put one hand to his upthrust head, scratching behind his small ears.

"Taggi?" Thorvald walked from the copter.

The wolverine slipped from under Charis's hand, went to the Survey officer. He sniffed inquiringly at the other's field boots, and then reared up against the man, his forepaws scraping Thorvald's thigh as he gave voice to a sound between a whine and a growl. There was no mistaking the questioning note, nor the demand for enlightenment which came to Charis mentally. Taggi wanted the one he knew better than Thorvald.

Charis sat where she was, cradling the nuzzling Tsstu close to her, but reaching out mentally to capture Taggi's thought stream, to try and tap that boiling and, to her, alien flow of brain energy. She touched and savored again, forcing herself not to shrink from the raw savagery, the strange stream. Taggi dropped on all fours. He was swaying from foot to foot, his blunt head swinging about so that he could eye her.

Thoughts—impressions like small sparks—whirled through the air above a stirred fire. Charis built up a picture of Shann Lantee within those sparks—Shann as she had seen him last on the hillside above the base.

Taggi came to her. His teeth closed upon the hand she held out in greeting, not with force enough to even pinch the skin but with the same caress of this kind that she had seen him give to Shann. And, too, inquiry—stronger and much more demanding.

Charis thought of the base as she had viewed it from the hill, knew that Taggi caught that. He dropped his hold upon her, turned halfway around to face in a new direction, and with his head up began sniffing the wind audibly.

Charis approached with some trepidation the real message she must pass along to the wolverine. Tsstu was much more in tune with her. How was she to project into that hunter's brain the sense of danger and an understanding of from whence danger came? By pictures of Shann as a prisoner?

First she thought of Lantee as he stood free by the pool. Then she added imagined bonds, cords about his wrists and ankles, to restrain his freedom. There was a loud snarl of rage from Taggi. She had succeeded so far. But caution! The wolverine must not race recklessly in under that prodding.

"—reeeeuuu—" Tsstu gave a cry Charis knew meant warning. The wolverine looked back at them.

Inquiry flashed not at her but at the curl-cat. The animals had their own band of communication. Perhaps that was her best answer.

Charis changed the direction of her warning, no longer striving to hold contact with the wild, rich stream of Taggi's thought, but to meet Tsstu's. Strike back against the enemy, yes; free Shann, yes. But for now, caution.

The rumbling growl from Taggi grew fainter. He was still shuffling impatiently from foot to foot, his eagerness to be gone plain to read, but Tsstu had impressed him with the need for caution and the old craftiness of his breed was now in command. Wolverines have great curiosity, but they also have a strong instinct for self-preservation; they do not walk easily into what might be a trap, no matter how attractive the bait. And Taggi knew that he faced a trap.

Again Charis centered on Tsstu, thinking out as simply as she could her own plan for entering the base. Suddenly she looked to Thorvald.

"The nullifier—could it stop communication of mind with mind?"

He gave her the truth. "It could well be so."

The animals must remain outside. Tsstu—the curl-cat was small—she could act as liaison between the wolverine and the base.

"Meeerrreee!" Agreement in that and another swift tongue-tip touch on Charis's cheek.

The girl rose to her feet. "There's no sense in delaying any longer. Time to go." Putting down the curl-cat, she pulled the tie from her hair, shaking the loosened strands about her neck and shoulders. By the time she reached the base, her hair would be sufficiently wild-looking, filled with bits of leaf and twig. She could not tear the Wyvern material off her clothing, but earth stains would adhere to it and the crawling she had already done provided dirty blotches. There were raw and healing scratches on her arms and legs. She would well present the appearance of someone who had been lost in a wilderness for a time. Moreover, the nourishment given by the Sustain tablets had worn off so that she did not have to feign hunger or thirst; she felt them both.

"Take care—" Thorvald's hand went out, almost as if he would hold her back on the very edge of action.

The contrast between that simple warning and what might lie ahead of her suddenly seemed to Charis so funny that a small, strangled sound of choked laughter was her first answer. Then she added, "Remember those words yourself. If you're spotted by some air scout—"

"They might spot the copter, they won't sight me. I'll be ready to move in to you when I can."

That "when I can" rang in Charis's ears as she walked away. Better make that "if I can." Now that she was committed to the venture, every possible fear—the product of a vivid imagination—swirled about her. She concentrated instead on her memory picture of Sheeha. She had to be Sheeha now as far as the invaders at the base were concerned—Sheeha, a woman brought in by the traders to contact the Wyverns, one who had broken at that meeting with the alien power. She had to *be* Sheeha.

Taggi played guide and advance scout, leading her down from the heights where the copter had landed. Here on the lowlands the predawn was still dark and Charis found the going more difficult. Her hair caught in branches; she tore free, adding more scratches to those she already bore. But that was all to the good.

For a while she carried Tsstu, but as they drew near the base, both animals took to cover and Charis kept touch by mind instead of sight or hearing.

Sun made silver droplets of the bubble shelters as Charis lurched into the open ground around the base. There was no need for her to fake her fatigue, for now she moved in a half-fog of exhaustion, her mouth dry, her ribs heaving with every gasping breath she drew. She must indeed look what she claimed to be—a fugitive, half-crazed, struggling out of the wilderness of a hostile world to seek the shelter and comfort of her own kind.

There was an unsealed door in the second of the bubbles. Charis headed for that. Movement there—a man in yellow coming into the open, staring at her. Charis forced a cry which was really a dry croak and slumped forward.

Calls—voices. She did not try to sort them out just yet but concentrated on lying limply where she had fallen, making no answer when she was rolled over, raised, and carried into the dome.

"What's a woman doing here?" That was one voice.

"She's been bush-runnin'. Lookit how she's all scratched up and dirty. And that ain't no service uniform. She ain't from here. You tell the captain what just blew in?"

"She dead?" asked a third voice.

"Naw—just out on her feet. But where'n Dis did she spring from? Ain't no settlement on this planet—"

"In here, captain. She just came runnin' outta the brush. Then she sees Forg, gives a kinda yip, and falls on her face!"

The click-click of magnetic space-boot plates. A fourth man was coming in to where she lay.

"Off-worlder, all right"—the new voice—"What's that rig she's wearing? That's no uniform, she couldn't be from here."

"From the post maybe, captain?"

"From the post? Wait a minute. That's right. They did bring in a woman to try to contact the snake-hags. But no, we found her when we took over their ship."

"No, there was two women, captain. First one blew up on 'em—went clean out of orbit in her head. So they got 'em another one. And she wasn't there when we took over. What about the tape you found here—the one askin' help from the base? She could be the one who sent it. Got outta the post and started runnin'—"

There was a twitch at her tunic as if one of those gathered about her was fingering the material.

"This is the stuff those snake-hags use. She's been with them."

"Prisoner, eh, captain?"

"Maybe—or something else. You, Nonnan, get the medic over here. He'll bring her around and then we'll have some answers. The rest of you, clear out. She might talk better if she doesn't come to with all of you looking her over."

Charis stirred. She did not care for the idea of a Company-squad medic. Such an expert might use the tongue-loosening drugs she had no guard against. It would be well to regain consciousness before his arrival. She opened her eyes.

She did not have to counterfeit her shriek. That came naturally as she faced—not the Company officer she had expected—but a creature seemingly out of a nightmare. Leaning toward her was one of the male Wyverns, his snout mouth slightly open to display the fang-teeth with which he was only too generously armed, his slit-pupiled eyes measuring her with no friendly intent.

Charis screamed a second time and jerked her legs up under as she sat bolt upright, squirming as far from the Wyvern as she could manage to move on the cot where they had laid her. The creature's taloned paw swept out and down, wicked claws scraping the foam mattress only inches away from her body.

A very human fist connected at the side of that reptilian head, sending the Wyvern off balance, crashing back against the wall, and a human in uniform took his place. Charis screamed again and cowered away from the Wyvern who had righted himself and was now showing a lipless snarl of rage.

"Keep it off! Snake!" she cried, remembering Sheeha's name for the Wyverns. "Don't let it get me!"

The officer caught the native by his scaled shoulder and headed him out the door with a rough shove. Charis found herself crying, a reaction she did not attempt to control as she shrank against the wall of the room, drawing herself into as small a space as possible.

"Don't let it get me!" she begged as she tried to appraise the man who now faced her.

He was very much of a type, a Company officer in the mercenary forces. Charis had seen his like before in space-port cities, and she thought she dared not depend upon his being less shrewd than any space officer. His very employment on a grab action would make him suspicious of her. But he was fairly young and his attack on the Wyvern made her think that he might be a little prejudiced in her favor.

"Who are you?" The demand was rapped out in a tone meant to force a quick and truthful answer. And up to a point she could supply the truth.

"Charis—Charis Nordholm. You—you are the Resident?" He would believe that she was ignorant of his uniform, that she thought him a government man.

"You might say so. I'm in charge at this base. So your name is Charis Nordholm? And how did you come here to Warlock, Charis Nordholm?"

Not too much coherence in her answer, Charis decided. She tried hard to remember Sheeha. "That was a snake," she accused. "You have them here." She eyed him with what she hoped would register the proper amount of suspicion and fear.

"I tell you the native won't harm you—not if you're what you seem," he added the last with some emphasis.

"What I seem—" she said. "What I seem—I am Charis Nordholm." She held her voice to a colorless recitation of facts as if she repeated some hard-learned lesson. "They

—they brought me here to—to meet the snakes! I didn't want to come—they made me!" Her voice lengthened into a wail.

"Who brought you?"

"Captain Jagan, the trader. I was at the trading post—"

"So—you *were* at the trading post. Then what happened?"

Again she could give him part truth. Charis shook her head. "I don't know! The snakes—they gave me to the snakes—snakes all around—they got inside my head—in my head." She set her hands above her ears, rocked back and forth. "In my head—they made me go with them—"

The captain was on to that in a flash. "Where?" His demand was purposely sharp to penetrate the haze that he supposed held her.

"To—to their place—in the sea—their place—"

"If you were with them, how did you get away?" Another man had come into the room and started toward her. The captain caught him back as he waited alertly for her answer. "How did you get away from them?" he repeated again with an emphasis designed to rivet her attention.

"I don't know—I was there—then I was all alone—all alone in a woods. I ran—it was dark—very dark—"

The captain spoke to the newcomer, "Can you get her to make better sense?"

"How do I know?" the other retorted. "She needs food—water."

The medic poured from a container and held out the cup. She had to steady it in both shaking hands to get it to her mouth. She let coolness roll over her dry tongue. Then she detected a taste. Some drug? She might already have lost the game because she had no defense against drugs and she had finished the draft. As a cover she kept the cup to her lips as long as possible.

"More—" she pushed the cup at the medic.

"Not now, later."

"So—" the captain was eager to get her back to her story "—you just found yourself in a woods and then? How did you get here?"

"I walked," Charis replied simply, keeping her eyes on the cup the medic was now holding as if that mattered far more than the officer's questions. She had never tried to play such a role before and now she hoped that the picture she presented was a reasonably convincing one. "Please—more—" she appealed to the medic.

He filled the cup about a third and gave it to her. She gulped it down. Drug or not this *was* her proper action. Her thirst allayed, her hunger was worse.

"I'm hungry," she told them. "Please, I'm hungry—"

"I'll get her something," the medic volunteered and left.

"You walked," the captain persisted. "How did you know which way to walk—to come here?"

"Which way?" Charis returned to her trick of repetition. "I did not know the way—but it was easier—not so many bushes—so I went that way where it was open. Then I saw the building and I ran—"

The medic returned, to put into her hand a soft plasta-skin tube. Charis, sucking at its cone end, tasted the rich, satisfying paste it contained. She recognized it as the revive ration of a well-equipped base.

"What do you think?" the captain asked the medic. "Could she just head in the right direction that way? Sounds thin to me."

177

The medic was thoughtful. "We don't know how this Power works. They could have directed her, without her being aware of it."

"Then she's meant to be their key in!" The look the captain directed at Charis was now coldly hostile.

"No, any directive such as that would fail once she got within the Alpha-rim. If they gave her some such hypo-order, it won't work now. You've seen how the warriors are freed from control here. If the hags did have some purpose and pointed her at us, it's finished."

"You're sure of that?"

"You've seen it happen with the males. The control does not operate within the rim."

"So—what do we do with her?"

"Maybe we can learn something. She has been with them—that is obvious."

"Might be more your department than mine," the captain observed. "You can take her on with the other one. He still out?"

"I told you, Lazgah, he's not unconscious in the ordinary sense." The medic was clearly irritated. "I don't know *what* he is except still alive. So far he hasn't responded to any restorative. Such a complete withdrawal —I've never seen its like before."

"Well, at least she isn't like him. And maybe you can learn from her. Try to, and the sooner the better."

"Come." The medic spoke softly. He held out his hand to Charis.

She eyed him over the tube from which she was now sucking the last remnants of paste.

"Where?"

"To a good place, a place where you may rest, where there is more food—water—"

"Out there?" She used the tube to point to the door behind him.

"Yes."

"No. There are snakes there!"

"One of the warriors was here when she came to," the captain explained. "Sent her farther off the beam."

"No, no one will hurt you," the medic assured her. "I won't let them."

Charis allowed herself to be persuaded. That scrap of conversation about the "he" who was being treated—It must be Lantee!

XVII

FOUR ROOMS made up a small but very well-equipped medical unit for the base. The worst feature, as far as Charis was concerned, was the single door to the outside, a door by which a blaster-armed guard already sat. To be free one must pass him.

Now the medic shepherded her on, his hand under her arm half-steering, half-supporting her, and she made her survey of the quarters in a series of seemingly aimless stares. They came into the third room and that touch on her arm brought her to a halt. She swayed, put out a hand against the wall to steady herself, hoping that her start could be attributed to her dazed condition.

Lantee lay on his back on a narrow cot. His eyes were wide open, but his face had that same blankness it had worn when she had found him among the rocks. He had returned to the husk of a living being, his true identity missing.

"Do you know this man?"

"Know this man?" Charis repeated. "Who is he? Know nim—why should I—" Her confusion was the best act she could achieve. She knew the medic was studying her closely.

"Come on." He took her arm again, led her into the next chamber. Two more cots. He pushed her down on the nearest one.

"Stay here."

He went out, sealing the door behind him. Charis ran her hands through the wild tangle of her hair. They could be watching her even now via some visa system, so take no chances. Anyway, she was in the base, and so far their suspicions of her were only normal. But just in case there was a spy system, she lay back on the cot and closed her eyes.

Outwardly she was composed for slumber; inwardly her thoughts were busy. Lantee—what *had* happened to Shann? The first time he had been shocked into such a state by a blast of the Wyvern Power. But that was not in effect here, and those few words Charis had heard exchanged between the captain and the medic suggested that their prisoner's present withdrawal had not come as a result of anything they had done. They were baffled by it.

"Withdrawal" the medic had phrased it—a way of escape. Charis almost sat up, startled by what she thought was the answer. Lantee had chosen this as a way of escape! He had purposely retreated thus before they could use a scanner or a truth drug, fleeing back into the same blackness, really retreating into what might prove death. And the motive for such a choice must have been a very strong one.

The Power would not work inside this Alpha-rim, whatever *that* was. Charis's hand moved against her tunic, feeling the slight bulk of the plasta-board which was her key to the place where Lantee had fled, a key which she could not turn. She had found Lantee, or rather the shell which had encased him. She had yet to find the nullifier or work out a plan against it. Her self-confidence was failing fast.

This was always the worst, this striving to cultivate patience with every nerve in her hammering for action. She must first establish her character as a bewildered fugitive. So she forced herself to lie quietly although she longed to be across that small room, trying the door to see if it was lock-sealed.

It had been early morning when she had come here; now the invaders, both off-worlders and Wyvern males, would be astir. Not a good time to go exploring. Exploring! Charis summoned concentration, sent out a creeping thought—not backed by the Power, but on her own—striving to reach Tsstu. If this avenue of communication was also blocked by their Alpha-rim—

A mind touch lapped against her probe as delicately as if the curl-cat was here in the room to give her a tongue-caress. Charis knew a throb of excitement, that road was not closed! She had contact, faulty and wavering as it was, with the animals outside the base.

The Tsstu link was no longer a touch but a firm uniting, and then came the feral urge she associated with Taggi—and another! Lantee? No. This was not the passageway link, but a heightening of the Taggi strain—his mate, the female wolverine! A piece of luck Charis had not counted on.

Tsstu was trying to send a message, drawing upon the united power of the wolverines to give it added impetus. A warning? No, not quite that; rather a suggestion that any action be delayed. Charis caught a very fuzzy picture of a Wyvern witch mixed in that. The female Wyverns must be taking a hand as they had promised. Then just as Charis tried to learn more, the curl-cat broke contact.

The girl began to think about Lantee. It had taken the Power to reach him before—the Power plus her own will and that of the two animals. But there in the copter she alone had found him, and without consciously drawing on the Power. Now, if he remained too long in that black world, would he ever come forth again? A small fire could die to ashes, never to be rekindled.

Charis willed herself to think of a black which was the entire absence of any light, the swallowing dark from which her species had fled since first they had learned the secret of fire as a weapon against that which prowled in the shadows. Cold crept up her body, the dark gathered in— A spark far in the heart of that dark . . .

A wrenching at her, dragging her back. Charis moaned at the pain of that wrenching. She opened her eyes to look up into the slitted ones set in a reptilian face where a cruel satisfaction gleamed.

"Snake!" She screamed.

The Wyvern male grinned, obviously highly amused by her shock and terror. He caught at her tunics, his claws in the fabric drawing her to the edge of the cot. But as he raised a paw for another grip, his scaled palm spread wide and then contracted quickly as if it had touched fire. A thin cry had burst from the alien; he jumped away from her.

"What's going on here?" a human voice demanded.

Hands appeared on the Wyvern's shoulders as a figure loomed behind the native, dragging him back.

Charis watched the medic pull the Wyvern out of her room. Then she stumbled after—to see the guard come into Lantee's room and aid the medic in forcing the struggling native on, the warrior all the while uttering sharp, shrill cries. She paused at the foot of Lantee's cot as they disappeared toward the outer door.

Shann! She did not cry that aloud, and even as she made a plea of it in her mind, she knew that there would be no answer. But still she longed now for his support.

His eyes were wide open, but behind them was nothingness. She did not have to touch his limp hand to know that it could not grip hers.

The cries of the Wyvern did not grow fainter. Instead they were augmented outside by a growing chorus. There must be more of the natives gathering. Were the Company men in dispute with their allies?

Charis hesitated. She longed to go to the outer door to see what was going on, but that action would not fit her present role. She should be cowering, frightened to death, in some corner. She listened—the clamor was dying— Better get back to her own room. She scuttled back.

"You—" Captain Lazgah stood in the doorway, his shoulders blocking the medic, and the tone of his voice was a warning.

Charis sat up on her cot, her hands were in her hair as if she had been pulling at it. "The snake—" she took the initiative swiftly "—the snake tried to get me!"

"For good reason." Lazgah's quick stride brought him to the cot side. His fingers were steel-tight and punishing about her right wrist as he pulled her about to face him squarely. "You've been using those hags' tricks. Snake—

you're a snake yourself! Those bulls out there have good reason to hate such tricks—they'd like to get their claws into you. Gathgar says you've been working with the Power."

"That's impossible!" the medic cut in. "You've had the complete reading from sensatator since she's been here. There's no indication that anything registered. Gathgar knows that she's been with the females and he built up all this on that fact alone."

"What do we know about this Power anyway?" Lazgah asked. "Sure, there's only been negative register since she's been here. But she might have some way of blanketing reception on that. A scanner could give us the truth."

"You put a scanner on her now and you'll get nothing but a complete burn-out. She'll be another like that fellow in there. What good will that do?"

"Turn the bulls loose on her and we could learn something."

"What can you learn from the dead? They're worked up now to a killing rage. Don't hurry and maybe—"

"Don't hurry!" The captain made a noise not far removed from one of Taggi's snarls. "We don't have much time left. This one knows where those hags have their base. I say—get her under questioning and find that out. Then we move and move fast. We have our orders to cut all corners on this deal."

"Destroy what you want and what good will it do? Sure, you can probably blast your way in and burn out the opposition, but you know what we've learned so far. The Power doesn't work unless you have had the training. It may not operate for males at all. You have a woman here who's already been sensitized to it. Why not use her just as Jagan intended—to pick up the information you need? You won't get that by force—either against her or maybe against the Wyvern females."

Lazgah relaxed his grip on Charis. But he still stood over the girl, staring at her as if he could reach inside her skull by his will and bring her under control.

"I don't like it," he stated, but he did not protest further. "All right—but you keep an eye on her."

The captain tramped out. But the medic did not follow. It was his turn to favor Charis with a measuring survey.

"I wish I knew whether you are playing a game," he said, surprising Charis with his frankness. "Those hags can't possibly control you past the Rim. But—" He shook his head, more at his own thoughts than at her, and did not finish his sentence. Going out abruptly, he closed the seal again.

Charis continued to sit on the cot. The Wyvern male Gathgar had accused her of working with the Power, but she had not. At least not with the aid of the patterns, Wyvern-fashion. Could it be, Charis's hand went to the plasta-board under her tunic, that she did not need such an aid any more? Was what she had been doing here— her contact with Tsstu, the reach-for Lantee—an easier method of using the same force?

But if that were true, there was a way of using the Power which could not be affected by the nullifier. Charis blinked. That surmise opened up a whole new field of speculations. She could reach Tsstu, and Tsstu could link in turn with the wolverines. Suppose that Tsstu, the wolverines, Charis and Lantee could form a chain to break open the Alpha-rim of the enemy?

Lantee— Somehow her thoughts always returned to Lantee, as if the pattern which was not a pattern needed the element for which he stood—just like the time she could not remember the right design until Tsstu supplied the indentations in her drawing. Charis could not have explained why she was certain of this, but she was.

She lay back on the cot and closed her eyes. Lantee must be summoned out of hiding, be one with them again. Charis released a questing thought, spun it out and away from her as a fisherman might cast a line or as a com beam might search for another installation to activate. A Wyvern witch working under the Power would have been accurate in such a hunt. She herself, using the pattern, could have centered on Tsstu and been reasonably certain of a quick contact, but this blind seeking was a fumbling process.

Touch! Charis tensed. Tsstu! Now she must hold that contact, signal along it her need for energy reserves for the job to be done. But Tsstu was unwilling. It was as if she was in Charis's hand and wriggling for her freedom. But Charis kept the line taut, sent her determined demand along it. There—Taggi came in. The girl braced herself against the impact of the far more savage mind of the wolverine. Through Tsstu to Taggi went her call for strength and a mutual pointing of their combined wills. Lantee—Charis made that call into form—Lantee. Now a fourth will joined—Togi, the female linked with her mate. The thrusting leap of that striking back to Charis was like a blow.

The girl held that linkage intact for a long moment, as a climber might examine knotted ropes to be sure of his support before facing a dangerous mountainside. Now! The wills were a spear which Charis not only aimed for the throwing but followed in flight.

Into the black of the nothing-place, surely the strangest of those Otherwheres into which the Power of the Wyverns led, she was the point of a fiery arrow shooting on and on, seeking the spark of light there. Now it was before her, very low, an ember close to extinction. But the arrow which was Charis, Tsstu, Taggi, and Togi struck into its heart.

Around them whirled a wild dance of figures. From all the doorways they had come into the corridor to crowd about her. She could not flee from them lest the lifeline break. This was worse than the first time she had walked this forbidden way, for the thoughts and memories of Shann Lantee now gathered more substance in their shadows. Charis knew a terror which balanced her on the thin edge of sanity.

However, the chain held true and pulled her back until she lay again on the cot, aware of its support under her. The contacts broke, the wolverines were gone; Tsstu, gone.

"I am here."

Charis opened her eyes, but no one in a green-brown uniform stood beside her. She turned her head to face the wall which was still between them.

"I am—back."

Again that assurance, clear-cut as audible words but, in her mind, coming with the same ease as the Wyvern witches communicated.

"Why—" Her lips shaped that soundlessly to match the inquiry in her mind.

"It was that or face the scanner," he answered swiftly.

"And now?"

"Who knows? Did they take you, too?"

"No." Charis outlined what had happened.

"Thorvald here?" Lantee's thoughts dropped away and she did not try to follow deeper. Then he was back to communication level. "The installation we're after is in the main dome. They have it guarded by Wyvern males who are sensitive to any telepathic waves. And they will fight to the death to keep it in action and themselves free."

"Can we reach it?" Charis asked.

"Little chance. At least, I've seen none so far," was his disappointing answer.

"You mean it's impossible for us to do anything?" Charis protested.

"No, but we have to know more. They've stopped trying to rouse me. Perhaps that will give me a chance to make some move."

"The Wyvern male told them I am using the Power. But I haven't tried it with the pattern and it didn't register on some machine of theirs, so they didn't quite believe him."

"You did this—without a pattern?"

"With Tsstu and the wolverines, yes. Does it mean we don't really need a pattern? That the Wyverns don't need them? But why wouldn't it show up on their machine?"

"May hit another wave length," Lantee returned. "But if the Wyvern males pick it up, they may be more sensitive on other bands than their mistresses credit. I wonder if they could have some Power of their own but don't know how to use it. If they picked you up before—"

"Then this last call for you—they could—"

"Be really alerted now? Yes. Which shaves our time to act. I don't even know how many there are here at the base."

"The witches have promised their help."

"How can they? Any sending of theirs will fail at the Rim."

"Shann, the Wyverns control their males with the Power. And the male I saw here believes that I can use it here. Suppose we all link again. *Could* we control them inside the Rim?"

There was a moment of pause in the flow of thought and then he answered.

"How do we know what will work and what won't until we put it to the test? But I want to be ready to get out of here on my own two feet. And from here I can see a guard with a blaster at the outer door. We might be able to link against the Wyvern males, but I wouldn't swear we could link to take out an off-worlder who has never been sensitized to mental control."

"What do we do?"

"Link with the others. See if you can reach Thorvald so—" he ordered.

This time the first link was not Charis, but Lantee and his will strengthened hers in her search for the curl-cat. Tsstu replied with a kind of fretfulness, but she picked up the wolverines.

A line cast out, spinning . . . then the catch of response.

"Wait!" That caution came back link by link. "The witches are moving. Wait for their signal." Break off as the animals dropped contact.

"What can they do?" Charis demanded of Lantee.

"Your guess is as good as mine." He was tense. "The medic's just come in."

Silence. How well could he play *his* role, Charis wondered a little fearfully. But if the medic had given up hope of reviving the Survey man, he might not examine him too closely now. She lay listening for any sound which might come through the walls.

The door of her room opened and the medic came in with a tray on which there was food, *real* food, not rations. He put it down on a drop-table and turned around to look at her. Charis tried to look like one awakening from a nap. The man's expression was set and the motion with which he indicated the food was abrupt.

"You'd better eat. You'll need it!"

She sat up, pushing back her hair, striving to present bewilderment.

"If you're smart," he continued, "you'll tell the captain all about it now. He's an expert on grab raids. If you don't know what that means, you'll soon discover the hard way."

Charis was afraid to ask what this warning did mean. To cling to her cloak of being a dazed fugitive was her only defense.

"You can't hide it—not any longer. Not with a complete burn-out of the sensatator this time."

Charis tensed. The linkage—twice the linkage—had at last registered on whatever safeguard the invaders had mounted.

"So you do understand that?" The medic nodded. "I thought you would. Now, you had better talk and fast! The captain might just turn you over to the bulls."

"The snakes!" Charis found words at last. "You mean give me to the snakes?" She did not have to counterfeit her repulsion.

"That gets to you, does it? It should; they hate the Power. And they'll willingly destroy anyone who uses it if they can. So—make your deal with the captain. He's willing to offer a good one."

"Simkin!"

There was such urgency in that hail that the medic whirled to the door. There was a growing murmur of sound—some of it sharp, the rest shouting. The medic ran, leaving the door open. Charis was up and into Lantee's room instantly.

The hissing blatt-blatt of a blaster in action came now. And she had heard that claking before when the birds had hunted her along the Warlockian cliff.

Then, like a swifter beat of her heart, a pulse along all the veins and arteries of her body—

"Now!"

The signal was not spoken but to it all of Charis responded. She saw Lantee slide from the cot in one supple, co-ordinated movement—as ready as she.

XVIII

LANTEE WAVED Charis back and took the lead as they approached the outer door. The Company guard still stood there, his back blocking their passage, intent upon what was happening outside, his blaster drawn and moving as if he were trying to align its sights on some very elusive mark.

The Survey man crossed the anteroom with the caution of a stalking feline as the din outside covered any sound within. But some instinct must have warned the guard. He turned his head, sighted Lantee and, giving a cry, tried to bring his blaster up and around.

Too late! Just what Lantee did Charis was not sure. The blow he struck was certainly not any conventional one. As the guard crumpled, the blaster fell to the floor and skidded. Charis pounced and closed fingers about the ugly weapon. She tossed it, as she straightened, to Lantee and he caught it easily.

They looked out into a scene of wild confusion, though their view of it was limited to a small segment of the base. Men in yellow uniforms crouched under cover and laced the air with blaster rays, apparently trying to strike back at some menace in the sky. Two of the Wyvern males lay either dead or unconscious by the door of a dome to the right, across from the one in which Shann and Charis had been prisoners. And there were burned and blasted clakers littering the ground in all directions.

"There—" Lantee gestured to the dome by which the Wyvern bodies sprawled. "It's in there."

But to try to reach that would set them up as targets for the marksmen now concentrating on the clakers. The din of the attack cries was lessening; fewer bodies struck the ground. Charis saw Lantee's lips thin, his face assume a grim cast, and she knew he was tensing for action.

"Run! I'll cover you."

She measured the distance by eye. Not far, but at this moment that open space stretched as an endless plain. And the Wyvern males? Those in sight were motionless, but more could be inside that open door.

Charis gave a leap which carried her well into the open. She heard a shout and then the crackle of a blaster beam which was close enough to scorch her upper arm. She cried out, but somehow she kept to her feet and stumbled on into the door, tripping there over the body of a Wyvern. She sprawled forward into the interior, thereby saving her life as one of the murderous, saw-toothed spears flew past her. She rolled, coming up against the wall where she pushed up to look at her assailants.

Wyvern males—three of them, two still holding spears, one of whom raised his weapon with sadistic slowness. The Wyvern was enjoying her fear as well as the fact that he was now in command of the situation.

192

"Rrrrrrrruuggghhh."

The Wyvern, his spear almost ready to throw, snapped around to face the door. A snarling ball of fury burst through it to launch at the natives. They howled, thrusting wildly at the wolverine. But the animal, using the advantage of its surprise attack to break past them, disappeared into the next room.

"Charis! You all right?"

Shann dodged in. The fabric of his tunic smoldered at rib level and he beat at it with his left hand.

"Surprisingly bad shots for Company men," he commented.

"Maybe they've orders not to kill." Charis tried to match his composure. But though she was on her feet now, she kept her back to the wall, facing the Wyverns, amazed that they had not launched a spear as yet. The eruption of the wolverine into their midst had shaken them oddly.

Shann gestured the three aliens back with his ready blaster.

"Move!" he ordered curtly. And the wariness in their yellow eyes told the two off-worlders that the natives were well aware of the potency of that weapon.

They retreated from the small outer room into the main room of the structure. There had been a good-sized com unit in here, but one glance told Charis that it could not serve them, for the installation had been deliberately rayed with blaster fire until it was half-melted in more than one place.

But that was not all that was in the room. On a base improvised from packing boxes was an intricate machine giving off an aura of rippling light. And, standing about that, almost as if they were cold and were warming their chilled bodies, were six male Wyverns. Now spears were leveled—until they sighted the blaster Shann held.

"Kill!" The word was scorching hate in Charis's mind as it flashed from the warriors.

"And be killed!" Shann returned in the same mental speech.

The snouted, spike-combed heads bobbed. Their surprise, their unease close to the border of fear, played about them much as did the light that rippled from the machine they guarded.

Lantee could do just that—wipe out the Wyverns *and* the machine they were striving to shield with their bodies. In Charis's thought, the natives *were* ready to die in that fashion. But was that the only answer?

"There might be a better one." Shann's thought came in reply to hers.

"Kill!" Not from the Wyverns now, but clear and as a feral demand. Taggi emerged from under the wreckage of the com.

"Here!" The small black shadow which had just flitted in sprang at Charis. The girl stooped and gathered up Tsstu. From her arms the curl-cat regarded the Wyverns with an unwinking stare.

"We die—you die!"

Clear-cut that warning. But the Wyvern who had made it did not raise his spear. Instead he placed his four-digited hands on the installation.

"He means it." This time Lantee used audible speech. "There must be some sort of panic button in that that will blow up the whole thing if necessary. Move away!" He changed to mental order and gestured with the blaster.

Not one of the natives stirred, and their determination

not to yield to that command beat back at the off-worlders in a counterblast. How long could such a standoff continue? Charis wondered. Sooner or later the Company men would be in on this.

She put down Tsstu and went back to the anteroom, to discover that while she could close the outer door, there was no way to secure that portal. The palm lock which had once fastened it was now only a blackened hole in the fabric.

"Kill the witch one! With *you*, we shall bargain."

The thought was clear speech in her head as she re-entered the wrecked com room.

"You are as we. Kill the witch and be free!" The males appealed to Lantee.

Tsstu hissed, her ears flattened against her round skull as she backed to a stand before Charis. Taggi growled from where he accompanied Shann, his small eyes alight with battle anger.

The spokesman for the natives glanced at both animals. Charis caught the quiver of uncertainty in his mind. Shann the Wyvern could understand; Charis he hated since he classed her with his own females who had always held the Power. But this link with animals was new and so to be feared.

"Kill the witch and those who are hers." He made his decision, lumping the unfamiliar with Charis. "Be free again as now we are."

"Are you?" From somewhere Charis found the words. "Away from this room or from the base where this off-world machine cannot reach—are you then free?"

Stark, hot hate glowing at her from yellow eyes, a snarl lifting scaled skin away from fangs.

"Are you?" Shann took up, and Charis readily gave way

to his leadership. To the Wyvern males, she was a symbol of all they hated most. But Lantee was male and so to them not wholly an enemy.

"Not yet." The truth was hard to admit. "But when the witch ones die, then we shall be!"

"But there may not be a need for such killing or dying."

"What are you thinking of?" Charis asked vocally.

Lantee did not look at her. He was studying the Wyvern leader with intensity, as if he would hold the native in check by his will alone.

"A thought," he said aloud, "just a thought which might resolve the whole problem. Otherwise, this is going to end with a real blood bath. Now that they know what this machine can do for them, do you think the males will ever be anything again but potential murderers of their own kind? And we can destroy this machine—and them, but that will be a failure."

"Not killing?" The Wyvern's thoughts cut in. "But if we do not kill them while they may not dream us defenseless, then they will in time break us and once more use the Power against us."

"Upon me they used the Power and I was in the outer dark where nothing is."

The astonishment of the Wyverns was a wave spreading out to engulf the off-worlders.

"And how came you again from that place?" That the Wyvern recognized the site of Lantee's exile was plain.

"She sought me, and these sought me, and they brought me forth."

"Why?" came flatly.

"Because they were my friends; they wished me well."

"Between witch and male there can be no friendship! She is mistress—he obeys her commands in all things—or he is naught!"

"I was naught, yet here I am now." Shann sought Charis. "Link! Prove it to them—link!"

She tossed the mental cord to Tsstu, to Taggi, and then reached for Shann. They were as one and as one, Shann thrust at the Wyvern's consciousness. Charis saw the spokesman for the natives sway as if buffeted by a storm wind. Then the off-worlders broke apart and were four again.

"Thus it is," Shann said.

"But you are not as we are. With you, male and female may be different. True?"

"True. But also know this: as one, we four have broken the bonds of the Power. But can you live always with a machine and those who have brought you the machine? Can they be trusted? Have you looked into their minds?"

"They use us for their purposes. But that we accept for our freedom."

"Turn off the machine," Shann said abruptly.

"If we do, the witches will come."

"Not unless we will it."

Charis was startled. Was Lantee running his claims too high? But she had begun to understand what he was fighting for. As long as the cleft between male and female existed in the Wyvern species, there would be an opening for just such trouble as the Company men had started here. Shann was going to attempt to close that gap. Centuries of tradition, generations of specialized breeding, stood against his will. And all the terrors and fears of inbred prejudice would be fighting against him, but he was going to try it.

He had not even asked for her backing or consent, and she discovered that she did not resent that. It was as if the linkage had erased all desire to counter a decision she realized as right.

"Link!"

A crackling explosion, the stench of burning plasta-fab. The Company soldiers had turned blasters on the dome! What did Lantee propose to do about that? Charis had only time for one fleeting thought before her mind fell into place beside the others.

Again it was Lantee who aimed that shaft of thought, sent it out past the melting wall of the dome, straight at the enemy minds, open and ill-prepared for such attack. Men dropped where they stood. A still-spitting blaster rolled along the ground, spraying its deadly ray in a wave pattern along a wall.

Shann had had the courage to try that first gamble and he had won. Could he do the same again in the greater gamble he proposed?

The Wyvern spokesman made a slight motion with his hand. Those who walled the machine with their bodies stood away.

"That is not the Power as we know it."

"But it was born of that Power," Shann caught him up. "Just as other ways of life may issue from those now known to you."

"But you are not sure."

"I am not sure. But I know that killing leaves only the dead, and the dead may not be summoned back by any Power ever known to living creatures. You will die and others shall die if you take the vengeance you wish. Then who will profit by your dying—except perhaps off-world-ers for whom you do not fight in truth?"

"But you fight for us?"

"Can I hide the truth when we touch minds?"

That curious quiet came down as a curtain between the off-worlders and the Wyverns as the natives conferred among themselves. At last the spokesman returned to contact.

"We know you speak the truth as you see it. No one before has broken the bonds of the Power. That you have done so means that perhaps you can defend us now. We brought our spears for killing. But it is true that the dead remain dead, and if we make the killing we wish, we as a people shall die. So we shall try your path."

"Link!" Again the command from Lantee. He made a motion with his hand and the Wyvern pressed a lever on the installation.

This time they had not fashioned a spear of the mind-force but a barrier wall, and only just in time. As a wave of determined attack struck against it, Charis swayed and felt the firm brace of Shann's arm as he stood, his feet a little apart, his chin up—as he might have faced a physical fight, fist against fist.

Three times that wave battered at them, striving, Charis knew, to reach the Wyvern males. And each time the linkage held without yielding. Then they were there in person—Gysmay, her brilliant body-patterns seeming to flame in her terrible anger, Gidaya—and two others Charis did not know.

"What do you?" The question seared.

"What we must." Shann Lantee made answer.

"Let us have those who are ours!" Gysmay demanded in full cry.

"They are not yours but their own!"

"They are nothing! They do not dream, they have no Power. They are nothing save what we will them to be."

"They are part of a whole. Without them, you die; without you, they die. Can you still say they are nothing?"

"What say you?" The question Gidaya asked was aimed at Charis, not Shann.

"That he speaks the truth."

"After the manner of your people, not ours!"

"Did I not have an answer from Those Who Have Gone Before which you could not read, Wise One? Perhaps this is the reading of that answer. Four have become one at will, and each time we so will it, that one made of four is stronger. Could you break the barrier we raised here while we were one, even though you must have sent against us the full Power? You are an old people, Wise One, and with much learning. Can it not be that some time, far and long ago, you took a turning into a road which limited your Power in truth? Peoples are strong and grow when they search for new roads. When they say, 'There is no road but this one which we know well, and always must we travel in it,' then they weaken themselves and dim their future.

"Four have made one and yet each one of that four is unlike another. You are all of a kind in your Power. Have you never thought that it takes different threads to weave a real pattern—that you use different shapes to make the design of Power?"

"This is folly! Give us what is ours lest we blast you." Gysmay's head-comb quivered, the very outlines of her body seemed to shimmer with her rage.

"Wait!" Gidaya interrupted. "It is true that this dreamer has had an answer from the Rods, delivered by the will of Those Who Have Dreamed Before. And it was an answer we could not read, but yet it was sent to her and was a true one. Can any of you deny that?"

There was no answer to her demand.

"Also, there have been said here things which have a core of good thought behind them."

Gysmay stirred, none of her anger abating. But she did not render her protest openly.

"Why do you stand against us now, Dreamer?" Gidaya continued. "You, to whom we have opened many gates, to whom we gave the use of the Power—why should you choose to turn that same gift against us who have never chosen to do you ill?"

"Because here I have seen one true thing: that there is a weakness in your Power, that you have been blind to that which makes evil against you. As long as you are a race divided against itself, with a wall of contempt and hatred keeping you apart, then there is a way of bringing disaster upon your race. It is because you opened doors and made straight a road for me that I will to do the same for you now. This evil came from my people. But we are not all thus. We, too, have our divisions and barriers, our outlaws and criminals.

"But do not, I pray you, Wise Ones," Charis hastened on, "keep open this rift in your own nation so that outside ill can enter. You have seen that there are two answers to the Power on which you lean. One comes through a machine which can be turned on and off at the will of outsiders. Another is a growth from the very seeds you have sown, and so it is possible for you to nourish it also.

"Without this man I have only the Power you gave to my summoning. With him and the animals, I am so much the greater that I no longer need this." From her tunic Charis took the map sheet, holding it out so that the Wyverns could see the pattern drawn upon it. She crumpled the sheet and tossed it to the floor.

"This must be thought upon in council." Gidaya had watched that repudiation of the pattern with narrowed eyes.

"So be it," Charis affirmed, and they were gone.

"Will it work?" Charis sat in the commander's quarters of the base. A visa-screen on the wall showed a row of Wyvern warriors squatting on their heels, guards for the still dazed Company men who had been herded into the visitors' dome in temporary imprisonment, awaiting the arrival of the Patrol forces.

Lantee lounged in an Eazi-rest, far down on his spine, while across his outstretched legs sprawled two wolverine cubs now snorting a little from the depths of slumber.

"Talk out, won't you?" Thorvald snapped in exasperation as he looked up from the emergency com. "I pick up only a kind of buzzing in the brain when you do that and it's giving me a headache!"

Shann grinned. "A point to remember, sir. Do I think our argument will convince them? I'm not venturing any guesses. But the witches are smart. And we proved them flat failures, tackling them on their own ground. That rocked them harder than they've ever been, I imagine. Warlock's been theirs to control; with their Power and their dreams, they have thought themselves invincible. Now they know they are not. And they have two answers: to stand still and go under, or to try this new road you've talked about. I'll wager we may have a tentative peace offer first, then some questions."

"They have their pride," Charis said softly. "Don't strip that from them."

"Why should we wish to?" Thorvald asked. "Remember, we, too, have dreamed. But this is just why you will handle the negotiations."

She was surprised at the tone of his voice, but he was continuing. "Jagan was right in his approach, a woman must be a liaison. The witches have to admit that Lantee and, to a lesser degree, myself have some small claim on their respect, but they will be happier to have you take the fore now."

"But I'm not—"

"Empowered to act on a diplomatic level? You are. This mission has wide emergency powers, and you are to represent us. You're drafted, all of you—Tsstu and Taggi included—to conduct a treaty with the witches."

"And it will be a real treaty this time!"

Charis did not know how Shann could be so sure of that, but she accepted his confidence.

"Link!"

Automatically now she yielded to that unspoken order. It was a new pattern, flowing, weaving, and she allowed herself to be swept along, sensing there were treasures to be found so: the subtle skill and neat mind that was Tsstu, the controlled savagery and curiosity that was Taggi and sometimes Togi.

Then there was that other—closer in some ways, different in others, and fast becoming an undissolvable part of her—which was strength, companionship. Hand rising to clasp hand, falling away, but always there to reach and hold again when needed. This had she brought with her from the Otherwhere of the Wyverns and this she would need ever hereafter to be complete.

WINNER OF
THE HUGO AWARD
AND THE
NEBULA AWARD
FOR BEST
SCIENCE FICTION
NOVEL OF
THE YEAR

*045930	**Babel 17** Delany	$1.25
062190	**Big Time** Leiber	95c
106237	**City** Simak	$1.25
166413	**Dragon Masters** Vance **The Last Castle** Vance	95c
167023	**Dream Master** Zelazny	95c
172635	**Dune** Herbert	$1.50
196824	**Einstein Intersection** Delany	95c
249029	**Four For Tomorrow** Zelazny	$1.25
478024	**Left Hand of Darkness** LeGuin	$1.50
727826	**Rite of Passage** Panshin	95c
791723	**Swords and Deviltry** Leiber	$1.25
806935	**This Immortal** Zelazny	$1.25

Available wherever paperbacks are sold or use this coupon.

7D

EDGAR RICE BURROUGHS

*056531	Beyond the Farthest Star	95c
*092833	Cave Girl	95c
*218032	Eternal Savage	95c
468702	The Lad And The Lion	95c
470138	The Land of Hidden Men	95c
*470229	The Land Time Forgot	95c
*492934	The Lost Continent	95c
514026	The Mad King	75c
*535898	Monster Men	95c
*537027	Moon Maid	95c
*537522	The Moon Men	95c
544601	The Mucker	95c
*605634	The Oakdale Affair	$1.25
644831	Out of Time's Abyss	95c
*645119	Outlaw of Torn	95c
659433	The People Time Forgot	95c
718155	Return Of The Mucker	95c
*901926	The Wizard of Venus	95c

EDGAR RICE
BURROUGHS

ANDRE NORTON

Available wherever paperbacks are sold or use this coupon.

24J

ANDRE NORTON

....	696823	Quest Crosstime — 75¢
....	749820	Sargasso of Space — 95¢
....	756965	Sea Seige — 95¢
....	758318	Secret of the Lost Race — 75¢
....	759910	Shadow Hawk — 75¢
....	768028	The Sioux Spaceman — $1.25
....	775510	Sorceress of Witch World — 75¢
....	780122	Star Born — 95¢
....	780726	Star Gate — 95¢
....	781310	Star Guard — 95¢
....	781922	Star Hunter & Voodoo Planet — 95¢
....	784314	The Stars Are Ours — 75¢
....	787424	Storm Over Warlock — 95¢
....	808022	Three Against the Witch World — 95¢
....	812521	The Time Traders — $1.25
....	863217	Victory on Janus — 95¢
....	873216	Warlock of the Witchworld — $1.25
....	878728	Web of the Witch World — 95¢
....	897025	Witch World — 95¢
....	925511	The X Factor — 75¢
....	942524	Year of The Unicorn — 95¢
....	959619	The Zero Stone — 75¢

Available wherever paperbacks are sold or use this coupon.